ANGELS AND OMENS

TREASURE TRAIL - BOOK 4

MORGAN BRICE

eBook ISBN: 978-1-64795-094-1
Paperback ISBN: 978-1-64795-095-8
Angels and Omens, Copyright © 2026 by Gail Z. Martin.
Cover by Lou Harper and May Dawney.

Darkwind Press is an imprint of DreamSpinner Communications, LLC

ANGELS AND OMENS

TREASURE TRAIL - BOOK 4

Morgan Brice

ONE

ERIK

A cold draft made Erik Mitchell shiver, right before a glass tottered off the edge of the break room counter and shattered on the floor.

"Stop that," he said to the empty room. "What's wrong with you today?"

"What happened?" Susan Hendricks, his assistant, came in from where she was watching the store. She stopped in the doorway and saw the broken glass. "Oh dear. I'll get the dustpan." She headed for the closet.

"It's the ghosts. They're more restless than usual." Erik took the brush and pan from her and swept up the mess, then dumped it in the trash can. "Can you feel it?"

Susan frowned for a moment, taking stock. "I feel more jittery than usual, like I ate too much sugar. Does that count?"

"Everyone's different." Erik wasn't a medium, but he could sense ghosts and see them when conditions were right. "I feel like I'm in the room with someone who's wound up to the breaking point, only there's no one around."

"Is it a full moon? Isn't that supposed to power up ghosts?" Susan took back the brush and pan and put them in the closet.

"Among other things." Erik grabbed his cup of coffee and turned to give a stern look to the empty room. "Behave."

In response, the plastic bottle of dish soap fell into the sink, although it hadn't been near the edge.

"We haven't had any new pieces come in that you haven't vetted," Susan said as they walked back into the shop. Trinkets had a long and storied history in Cape May for being a place to find high-quality antiques or sell valuable heirlooms. It also had a well-established but quieter reputation for being the place to go to get help with cursed or haunted objects.

Sometimes taking in an object that had supernatural residue without containing it properly led to an unruly spirit or bad energy. "Anything that might be a problem is warded and in the safe," Erik replied. "But I've been feeling drafts all morning, and I can sense presences even if I can't see or hear them."

"Give Monty a call." Susan named a friend who was a spirit medium. "He can probably tell you if there's a bad moon on the rise, and stop in to send the spooks on their way."

"We usually don't have any problem with the long-timers," Erik mused. The shop had a long history of handling magical, cursed, haunted, and supernatural objects. A few ghosts chose to hang around, and Erik didn't mind so long as they didn't cause damage or upset customers or staff.

"Then there's probably something going on," Susan replied. "He'll know."

Susan stayed up front in case a customer walked in, and Erik returned to the break room for privacy and placed the call.

Monty Clark answered on the second ring. "Hey, Erik. What's up?"

"Hi, Monty. Is there a reason the ghosts are restless? The shop spirits are usually quiet, but they're in a mood today."

"I've heard that from a lot of people recently, and we're seeing that here at the lighthouse. Even Jon is fidgety." Monty was the resident keeper of the Cape May Light, where he lived with his ghostly lover, Jon.

"Does Jon know why?"

"No, and that worries me a little," Monty said. "It's more than the usual full moon energy. My bet is that either someone with strong psychic abilities just came to town, or there's a new object that is causing the effect. But those are just educated guesses. I'm sorry that I don't have answers."

"I know you can't leave the lighthouse," Erik said. "Is there someone you recommend who might be able to get our ghosts to chill a little?"

"Actually, yes," Monty said. "Haley Connor. She moved to Cape May a few months ago, and she's a very gifted—and powerful—spirit medium. She's the real deal. Séances, dispelling troublesome ghosts, un-haunting objects."

"Sounds perfect," Erik replied. "If she checks out with you, that's good enough for me."

"She gave me a business card. Here's her scheduling number." Monty read off the digits, and Erik made a note. "Tell her I sent you."

"Will do. Hope you and Jon have a good evening," Erik said as he ended the call and entered Haley's number.

He was surprised when Haley picked up right away. "Spirited Outlook, this is Haley Connor. How can I help you?"

"I'm Erik Mitchell at Trinkets. Monty Clark recommended you. We don't usually have a problem with our resident ghosts, but they've been unsettled today, and I was hoping that you could help."

"It's been quite the day for that," Haley said. "And before you ask, I don't know what's got the spirits riled up, but it's widespread. Are you in danger?"

Erik took a few seconds to read his intuition. "I don't think so, but there's been some breakage, and that's bad in an antique store."

"I understand. If you can hang in there for an hour, I've got a break between appointments. You're not far away. I'll pop over and see if I can help. In the meantime, if you have a lavender or sandalwood candle handy, those scents can help soothe restless spirits."

"Will do," Erik said. "Thank you so much. See you soon."

He relayed the information to Susan, then returned to the break room, took a pillar candle out of the cupboard, and lit it in the sink where it wouldn't cause damage if it got knocked over.

"You are welcome to stay here, but please don't cause trouble," Erik said to empty air. The ghosts' presence was strong enough that he could sense it. "And if there's danger, tell Haley when she comes."

Nothing stirred, and Erik hoped his message had been received.

"If you don't need me up front, I'll stay in here with my laptop until Haley arrives," Erik told Susan, reluctant to leave the candle unattended. "Just in case."

"That's fine," she said. "It's been quiet so far."

Erik settled in at the table and went back to work on invoices and orders. The candle's scent filled the air, and whether or not it was calming the ghosts, he found it soothing.

The hour flew by, and Erik looked up when he heard the bell jangle to indicate a new arrival.

"Erik, this is Haley. Haley, Erik," Susan introduced a few minutes later.

"Monty told me you might be in touch." Haley stepped forward to shake his hand. She looked to be in her early thirties with short blond hair and bright green eyes.

Erik chuckled. "Actually, it doesn't surprise me that Monty figured we'd connect."

"He told me a little about your work and some of the situations you and your partner have handled recently. Never a dull moment!" she added.

"I wouldn't mind duller moments, but loose ends seem to find us," Erik replied. "Trinkets isn't just an antique store. Part of our founding mission was to get haunted and dangerous objects out of the wrong hands. Antiques come with a lot of emotional resonance and more than a few ghosts. I have a contact who safely removes the most dangerous pieces, but it would be great to help the spirits move on and un-haunt the pieces, so I suspect you'll hear from me often."

"Believe it or not, I've worked with museums and antique shops more than a few times." A loud boom of thunder drowned out Haley's words.

"Our resident ghosts are usually well-behaved," Erik said. "And the shop itself is heavily warded. That's why having them act up worries me. I'm sorry to bother you."

She made a dismissive gesture. "Not a problem. Glad to help."

Haley walked into the break room and stopped after a few steps. She closed her eyes and seemed to be listening intently.

"I know you're here," she said quietly. "Something has upset you. I'm sorry about that. I can't make whatever it is stop, but I can help you mind it less. If I do that, will you stay quiet and not break anything else?"

Haley nodded, responding to voices only she could hear. "Good. I will take your word on that."

She opened her eyes and looked at Erik. "It helps to have someone acknowledge that you're upset, even after you're dead."

Haley set her messenger bag on the table and took out a few containers, a bowl, and a pestle. She combined several powders and a sweet-smelling liquid in the bowl and then let the mixture fall drop by drop into the candle flame.

"No harm will come to you within these wards," Haley said. "Whatever you sense elsewhere cannot reach you. Be at peace, and do not trouble the things or people in this building." She blew out the candle and watched the rising spiral of smoke. .

Erik didn't see or hear anything, but the jangly feeling eased, and he hoped that meant that the spirits could relax and ignore whatever had provoked them.

"Thank you," he told Haley after she packed up her materials. "What do I owe you?"

"First one's on the house," she replied with a laugh. "I have the feeling we'll be working together a lot."

He thanked her again and walked her to the door. "If you find out what's stirring them up, let me know," Erik reminded her.

"I will definitely keep you on speed dial," Haley assured him, and left with a wave to Susan.

Erik remained at the window for a few minutes, looking out onto the street. The gloomy day threatened rain, although it had only delivered intermittent showers and some thunder.

"Something interesting?" Susan came up to stand beside him. She was the mother of the Cape May chief of police and close in age to Erik's own mom.

"It's not just our ghosts who are upset. Even if I can't see them, I know the local spirits are jittery."

Cape May, New Jersey, was famous for its history, architecture, and haunted places. While visitors enjoyed ghost tours and the occasional sighting, to those who lived here, the spirits were just a different kind of neighbor.

"You have a two o'clock appointment coming up," Susan reminded him. "Mr. Thompson has an antique ring he wants to get appraised for sale."

"Did he say anything else about it?" Erik asked. Sometimes the antiques they handled came without supernatural baggage, but more often than not, the pieces had a hidden story and a complicated past.

"Just that he was hoping to come to an agreement today. I guess he needs the money." Susan shrugged.

Or it's causing him trouble, Erik thought.

By the time Thompson arrived, Erik was ready. He decided to err on the side of caution and assume the ring was actively or maliciously haunted. That meant doing the appraisal warded against dark supernatural energies.

Erik had also set out a cloth on the table that was blessed and woven with silver threads, and had a pair of gloves made of the same material so he didn't have to handle the ring with bare skin. A box covered with protective runes sat nearby, ready to hold the ring until Erik could put it in the spelled safe for one of his contacts to deal with safely.

A thin, middle-aged, balding man entered the shop and glanced around. He looked haggard and his clothing was rumpled and coffee-stained. His gaze settled on Erik. "Are you the owner? I'm Bill Thompson."

Erik nodded. "I'm Erik Mitchell. Please, come in." He ushered

Thompson into the break room and gestured for him to sit down at the table across from the protective cloth.

"Tell me about your ring," Erik said.

Thompson glanced from side to side as if he were afraid of being overheard. "You're going to think I'm nuts."

"I promise that I won't," Erik assured him. "You'd be surprised at what items come into an antique shop, especially one like ours."

"I heard that you handle *problem* pieces. Is that true?"

Erik shrugged. "I guess it depends on the type of problem. Haunted or with a tinge of supernatural energy, yes. Questionable provenance or uncertain legality, no."

"It's not stolen," Thompson said hurriedly. "Nothing like that. But ever since I brought the damn thing home, it's been like one of those poltergeist movies. Things move from place to place on their own. Books fall over when no one's near. A coffee cup exploded. And I feel like I'm being watched."

Thanks to Haley just cleansing the area and strengthening the protections, those effects were muted, but Erik once again sensed nearby spirits that were much less agreeable than the shop's resident ghosts.

"What would you like to do?" Erik asked.

"Throw it in a volcano, like in that movie," Thompson replied without humor. "Sell it to you if you'll buy. I'd be happy to get a fraction back of what I paid just to be rid of the damn thing."

"Go ahead and set the ring on the cloth," Erik instructed as he pulled on the gloves. "I can't resell it. But I can make sure it doesn't hurt anyone else."

The ring tumbled out of the box Thompson withdrew from his pocket, a pretty circlet of silver with tiny carved runes that Erik was certain invoked magic of some sort. It was old but not particularly valuable for craftsmanship, although he wondered about the provenance.

Erik quickly put the ring into the spelled containment bag and felt the energy in the room ease. "Do you know anything about its history?"

Thompson shook his head. "No. I saw it at a swap meet that I went to a few days ago. A lady with a table had all kinds of baubles, and it caught my eye. I asked about it because it looked old, and she said it had belonged to several powerful women in her family, and it was time to pass it on."

"Did you get a business card?" Erik asked, although he suspected he already knew the answer.

"No. It was an impulse buy. And when the weird things started to happen and I went back, she was gone, and no one knew how to contact her," Thompson said ruefully.

"She took advantage of you. It's not your fault," Erik said. "I'll make sure the ring never causes problems for anyone else."

"How much can you give me for it?" Thompson asked.

Erik shook his head. "I can't resell it, so I can't pay you for it. But I can dispose of it safely and permanently."

Thompson bit his lip, clearly having a silent argument with himself. Finally, he sighed.

"Then take it. I'd be willing to pay you to get rid of it."

"Not necessary," Erik assured him. "That's part of what we do. But when you go home, open the windows, burn a candle, and say a blessing or a prayer of protection. If there's any bad mojo left behind, that will help get rid of it. And if it doesn't, my friend Haley can help. Susan can give you her contact information."

"Thank you," Thompson replied, and Erik wondered if the man had slept since he acquired the ring.

"Glad we could be of help." Erik walked him back to Susan, and wasn't surprised when she gave the man one of Haley's business cards from a new stack by the register.

"I figured the cards would come in handy," she said when Thompson left.

"Good thinking. I suspect we'll be doing a lot of business with Haley." Erik went back to the break room to retrieve the bag and stashed it in the safe before removing the gloves and putting his other supplies away.

———

"Looks like we're in for a big storm." Monty Clark, keeper of the Cape May lighthouse, settled his six-foot-four-inch frame on the picnic table bench near the base of the tower. "Thanks for stopping in before the weather gets crazy." He ran a hand through his black hair to tame it from the wind.

"Figured you could use the caffeine." Erik nodded toward the carrier of large coffee cups in the middle of the table. He and his partner Ben Nolan had picked up coffee and freshly baked cookies on their way to the visit.

"Definitely." Monty reached for the cup and let out a hum of satisfaction at the first swallow. Then he glanced at the seat beside him. "Get your mind out of the gutter," he said to his ghostly partner, Jon.

Erik chuckled. He and Ben could sometimes see and occasionally hear ghosts if they were strong enough to manifest, and Jon usually made himself visible for at least part of the time when they visited.

The wind gusted, and Erik tucked a strand of blond hair out of his blue eyes.

"You need a haircut," Ben joked. His dark hair was cut in a fade, too short to be bothered much by the stiff breeze.

"You like my hair," Erik retorted with a knowing look, thinking of the way Ben had tugged on it the night before in bed.

Ben returned a naughty smile. "Sure do."

Erik grew serious and looked to Monty. "Do you have everything you need to ride out the weather?"

Monty nodded. "Yes, thanks for asking. I always have some food and drinks stockpiled and a generator, if things get really bad. They're not calling for a full hurricane, so I'm hoping we don't get anything too dramatic. Jon's good company." Monty nodded at a spot next to him, and Jon faded in and out.

Jon Richards was a stuntman who died seventy years ago and chose never to move on to whatever came next. Jon and Monty had become friends and then partners. Erik didn't completely understand how their relationship worked, but he figured all that mattered was that they were happy together.

"Jon says it's not just the storm. The ghosts are restless," Monty told them.

"Because of the weather or something else?" Erik asked.

"Like we talked about before, Jon acknowledges that something's up," Monty replied. "But he doesn't know what, just that it's not good. He says he's seen a woman in white a couple of times."

"Bad omen," Erik said. "But about what?"

"Is there a significant anniversary of some disaster coming up?" Ben pulled out his phone and did a quick search. Cape May's storied history made for a long list of results.

Monty cocked his head as he listened to the reply. "The *SS Mohawk* went down in a bad storm. Might be from that," Monty repeated what Jon told him. Over the decades since his death, Jon had befriended other ghosts who still retained a sense of self. Some he helped to pass on, while he kept track of others who wanted to remain. More than once, Jon had used the strength he had gradually gained as a spirit to save people from drowning or sinking boats.

"I read about that," Erik chimed in. "Back in the 1920s. Passenger liner—something in the hold caught fire. But the article I read said that while the boat was a loss, no one died."

"She was a stowaway." Monty looked surprised as he relayed Jon's comment.

"Do you know her name?" Monty asked.

"Lila. That's all she remembers," Monty repeated Jon's answer.

"I thought a woman in white was an omen but not necessarily the ghost of a real person," Ben said.

"There are hundreds of stories, and they don't all match." Erik shrugged. "That's the tough part about the lore. Look into the *Mohawk's* history. If it's showing up now, maybe there's a story we've missed."

"I don't remember that particular ship causing trouble," Monty said. "I've heard divers say it's a dangerous wreck because of the current. It's been a hundred years, so maybe the anniversary is giving

Lila a boost." He paused. "I've tried to make contact with Lila's ghost and see if I could send her on, but there's something blocking me. Makes me wonder if there was some sort of magic involved."

"Magic?" Ben echoed.

Monty shrugged. "Lila appears to be the only ghost from the wreck. If she worked a desperate spell trying to save herself or the ship, it might not have gone as intended."

"Interesting angle." Erik was already thinking of possibilities.

Monty sipped his coffee. "Other than the storm, are things staying quiet for the two of you?"

Erik nodded. "For now—don't jinx us. We could use some downtime."

"Better get some rest before the festival plans ramp up," Monty warned. "You know what a big deal that is."

Erik and Ben both nodded, and Ben groaned. "Yeah, we know. Great for tourism, and a ton of work to prepare." The Awesome Autumn Festival created a week-long celebration with plenty of special events, with participation by the town's Arts Council and business owners.

"Still beats the downsides of my old job," Erik joked.

Before he moved to Cape May and bought Trinkets, an antique and curio shop, Erik had used his expertise in art to travel the world helping museums and law enforcement find stolen masterpieces and stop smuggling rings. That had earned him powerful enemies, including Bratva, the Russian Mob.

Ben had been a Newark cop and private investigator before he came to Cape May to take over his aunt and uncle's rental real estate company. He had been involved in several high-profile busts that involved the Newark Mafia, a group with a long memory.

Despite Erik and Ben trying to stay low-profile, old cold cases often attracted the notice of bad guys who wanted to elude authorities. Erik's abilities as a psychometric to read the history of objects by touch and Ben's sleuthing talents had landed them in hot water a couple of times when scandals and murders meant the past refused to stay buried and forgotten.

"Even if Lila was a stowaway and her death wasn't counted with the *Mohawk* sinking, if I can find out a last name, maybe we can figure out who she was and help her move on," Erik said.

This time the wind nearly took their cups off the table, and the sky had grown darker.

"Guess it's time for me to go back to work." Monty stood. "Thanks for the visit. Best go straight home. This storm isn't going to be anything to fool with."

"Sometimes a ghost is just a ghost," Ben said as they headed for Erik's SUV.

"Yeah, but if Jon says Lila is an omen, then there's more to the story aside from her death," Erik countered. They barely made it into the Highlander before the rain started, pelting the windshield with fat drops.

"Admit it, you're bored and looking for the next case." Ben gave a fond grin as he reached over to rest his hand on Erik's thigh as he drove.

"Busted," Erik replied. "And maybe for once, this one won't have any ties to organized crime."

"When did we ever get that lucky? After all, this is Jersey," Ben replied.

Erik had already called Susan and told her to go home before the storm broke. They were unlikely to get any customers in a raging thunderstorm, and at least she would get home without being soaked.

That also meant unlocking the door in the rain once they arrived. Ben ran ahead with the key and an umbrella as soon as Erik parked. Erik followed, holding the hood of his rain jacket tight against the wind. Neither man stayed completely dry, but they weren't wet to the skin, so Erik counted it as a win.

He turned on the lights and went to the kitchen to make a fresh pot of coffee, since they had both finished their takeout lattes.

Ben got his laptop and sat at the table. "I'm going to see what I can find about that shipwreck. It's a long shot trying to find out more about Lila, but sometimes I get lucky."

"I can help you get lucky," Erik teased with a smirk.

"Hold that thought," Ben replied. "I'm all for it."

Moving in together was relatively recent, and the shift had gone smoother than either man dared hope. Ben had been living in one of the rental units for Nolan Rental Real Estate, the company he took over for his aunt and uncle when they retired. Erik had the apartment above Trinkets, which was big enough for both of them. Erik loved the new arrangement, and Ben swore he was happy with it too.

"While you do that, I'm going to look at the inventory list," Erik said. "The SS *Mohawk* sounds familiar."

As soon as the coffee finished brewing and they both had fresh steaming cups, Erik went to his office and pulled up the files he needed. Trinkets added to their supply of antiques and collectibles almost daily, between what people dropped by to sell and what Erik acquired online and at estate sales.

He started searching on the *Mohawk* and found several similarly-named ships that had all come to a bad end. Monty had said that Lila's unlucky craft had gone down in the 1920s, so that helped eliminate the false leads. It also meant that divers and ocean currents had a century to strip away anything that survived the fire and the crash onto the bottom of the ocean.

Being a psychometric who could sense the energy and history of objects by touching them, Erik carefully curated the pieces he sold in the shop to do no harm. Those that radiated malevolence or bad magic, he secured and sent to a contact in Charleston equipped to cleanse or destroy them.

Even so, the nature of old things meant they had absorbed a lot of the emotions and memories of the people who had owned them and the history they had witnessed, often leaving a bittersweet resonance. Some buyers seemed attuned to those vibes even if they couldn't have explained what they sensed, while others were blissfully unaware.

Erik worked his way through the inventory, glad that the prior owner had been meticulous about record-keeping. That meant he could see what items had come through the store, both past and present.

"There it is." Erik spotted the doomed ship's name and pulled up the records.

"Find something?" Ben walked out of the kitchen cradling a cup in his hands. He came around to look over Erik's shoulder at the screen.

"Yeah, I thought it sounded familiar." Erik pointed to the items that had popped up. "Monty mentioned it.

"The *Mohawk* burned and sank, but small items washed ashore in the days and weeks afterward. An old man collected them and eventually sold the collection to Trinkets. Somehow a cup and saucer with the ship's logo survived," Erik marveled. "Along with a salt shaker and a handful of old buttons."

"That's a tie to the ship itself, but not to Lila," Ben said. "And if the items are inside the store's protections, it's probably not what's anchoring her ghost, especially since she's haunting places outside the store."

Erik nodded. "I agree. But it might be enough for Alessia to test our theory about magic being involved in the sinking. If she can figure out what happened, she might be able to neutralize what remains of the spell. Monty's a strong medium, but he isn't a witch."

"Did you sell the pieces, or are they still in storage?" Ben leaned closer for a better look at the photos.

"Storage." Erik jotted a note to himself on his phone. "They came in right before the store was sold, and I'm guessing it just wasn't a priority to deal with them." He looked up at Ben. "How about you?"

Ben grinned. "I think I've found our woman in white."

Erik followed him back to the kitchen and pulled up a chair next to where Ben sat in front of his laptop.

"The *Mohawk* sailed from Boston to New York, then down to Charleston and Jacksonville with passengers and cargo, before turning around and doing the whole trip in reverse," Ben told him. "There was a bad storm the night the *Mohawk* sank, but what doomed it was a fire in the cargo hold. Other ships got the passengers to safety, but all the cargo was lost, and the ship burned to the waterline before it sank," Ben said.

"What about Lila?" Erik leaned in for a better look at Ben's screen.

"There's no Lila on the passenger manifest," Ben said. "If she was registered, that wasn't her legal name. Since the official account says all the passengers were saved, I think she must have been a stowaway, like Jon said."

"That's going to make it tough to find out who she was," Erik replied.

Ben nodded. "I know. I did a search on missing women named Lila in the ports where the *Mohawk* stopped in the year it sank. She could have come from other places, but I had to narrow down the search."

"That was a hundred years ago. If she wasn't famous, no one might have noticed that she went missing," Erik said. "And the records are spotty."

"True. But I think I got a break." Ben brought up a new screen and pointed to what was posted.

"Delilah McIntosh, also known as Lila, daughter of a prosperous banker in New York, was reported missing right before the *Mohawk* incident. The article leaves it open to whether she ran away or was kidnapped, but there was a reward offered for information and for returning her safely to her family," Ben said.

The grainy black-and-white photograph of a young woman in her twenties came up on the screen.

"Because her family was well-off, the story got picked up by other papers," Ben said. "One of her friends was quoted as saying that she had met a man from Charleston and fallen in love with him against her family's wishes, and that they planned to run away together when she disappeared."

"You think she was going from New York to Charleston on the *Mohawk* and stowed away so her family couldn't find and stop her?" Erik asked.

"Seems likely," Ben replied.

Outside, the wind howled and rain came down in sheets, tapping against the store's big front windows.

"I think the *Mohawk* items are in the storage area in the back room," Erik said. "If not, we'll have to wait out the storm before we go to the offsite unit."

"Why don't you call Alessia and see if she can check if there's magic involved? If that doesn't work, we can see if Haley would help dispel Lila's spirit."

"I've been thinking the same thing," Erik replied. "I'll call her, and then see if I can find the items from the *Mohawk*."

"Not going anywhere else tonight," Ben said. "I'll start thinking about what we've got on hand to make dinner."

Erik pulled up Alessia's contact information on his phone and figured she would probably be home, given the bad weather. Alessia Mason was a friend of theirs and a powerful witch. She ran the local coven as well as the Spirit of the Sea gift shop, and her marriage into an old, prominent Cape May family provided a degree of social protection beyond what her magic afforded.

For as strong as her magic was, Alessia wasn't a medium like Monty or Haley, since she could see and hear ghosts but not summon them. She could, however, use magic to help send them on.

"Erik, what's up?" Alessa greeted him.

"First off, thanks for introducing me to Haley. She's terrific, just helped me out on a haunted item," Erik said. "I'm sure we'll do a lot of business together—you know how Ben and I keep finding haunted stuff." Erik had been thinking for a while that, for as often as solving the complicated history of the antiques that came into Trinkets, having a connection to another medium would come in handy, so he was happy to have found Haley.

"Not to mention dead mobsters," Alessia snarked, recalling some of their recent incidents.

"That, too," Erik replied with a sigh.

"Haley's pretty new in town, and she's the whole enchilada," Alessia replied. "She can also do séances, dispel troublesome ghosts, and, as you now know, remove haunts from objects."

"I'm curious. What brought her to Cape May?" Erik asked.

"She's a historian, and she's working on a grant-funded project for the library and the Historical Society," Alessia replied. "The project entails having her interview ghosts about local history to capture what they know before they fade. Of course, it will be in a special collection with limited access because that kind of thing isn't common knowledge, but I'm really interested to see what she comes up with."

"Where did the funding come from?" Erik was equally fascinated by the project concept.

"The Fox Institute in Upstate New York," Alessia said. "It's a scholarly organization dedicated to the paranormal. Very legit."

"I'm sure we'll need her help quite a bit. Although the backstory for the ghosts might involve some unsavory information," Erik warned. "I hope that won't bother her."

Although Erik and Ben had retired from active law enforcement, cold cases kept finding them, and many of those involved the Mafia.

"I don't think it will," Alessia said with a laugh. "She's been an off-the-books consultant to several police departments when they hit a brick wall on investigations. They can't fess up to having someone talk to ghosts to get information, but when a lead from a confidential informant breaks a case, they don't have to."

"Interesting. Most cops I've met are skeptics, if not outright hostile to spooky stuff." Erik couldn't help thinking about Cape May's own Chief Cole Hendricks, who definitely mistrusted anything he deemed to be "woo-woo."

"I'm glad Haley was able to help you. But I doubt that's why you called," Alessia said.

Erik filled her in on the relics from the *SS Mohawk* and Lila's ghost, as well as their theory that misguided magic might have trapped the spirit with the wreck. "If it quits storming tomorrow, would you be able to stop in and see if you can sense any magic involved? If there's a spell gone wrong, maybe it can be broken to send her on."

"Let me check my schedule. You might want to include Haley as well." She paused for a moment. "Nine a.m. work? Meet you at Trinkets?"

"That works great, and I'll call Haley next," Erik told her. "I'll have coffee ready. Thank you so much." He felt relieved to have a plan and called Haley before getting a fresh cup of coffee and joining Ben.

"I found more about Lila online," Ben took a seat across from Erik at the table. "Her family offered a reward for information and reported her missing to the police. I think they were afraid she'd been kidnapped. A few years later, there was an obituary notice that said 'missing, presumed dead.' I don't think they ever realized she was on the *Mohawk*."

"I'm guessing her parents either opposed the marriage or the man she loved, and Lila took matters into her own hands," Erik said. "It's too bad she didn't get her happy ending."

Erik's phone rang, and he saw that it was Susan. "Hi Susan, is everything okay?"

"Yeah, just a little damp. I wanted to remind you to look at the event checklist email for Awesome Autumn, which should be in your inbox. They'll probably want you to do a couple of programs about antiques, and for Ben to talk about architecture and old houses like last year."

Erik glanced at Ben, who had heard what she said and nodded.

"That should be fine, but we'll look at it first thing tomorrow," Erik promised. "We had fun last year, and the event brought in a lot of new visitors, all for a good cause."

"I was hoping you'd say that. I'll see you tomorrow if we don't float away before then," Susan added before ending the call.

Rapping at the door jerked both men to attention. "Who would be out in this weather?" Ben asked as Erik rose to look out the window by the door.

Although they were technically closed, Erik had turned on the lights so the man on the front step could be forgiven his mistake. He shifted from one foot to the other as he stood beneath an umbrella, holding a large square picture box.

"I've got your back." Ben moved to stand beside the desk, where Erik kept a gun. All their run-ins with the Mob made it prudent to take precautions.

Erik's intuition told him to meet with the stranger. He opened the door and motioned for the man to come inside. It wasn't raining quite as hard anymore, but the man still looked soggy. Whatever he wanted was urgent enough to send him outside in the storm.

"Thanks." The man stomped his feet, peeled off his soaked rain jacket, and hung it on the doorknob. He was a bedraggled middle-aged man with thinning hair and a lean build, suggesting that he had been a runner in his younger years.

"It's a nasty night to be out and about," Erik observed. "I'm Erik Mitchell, and I own the shop. This is my partner, Ben. How can I help you?"

"I'm Peter Randolph," the man said. "Do you believe in ghosts?" His question held a note of desperation.

"What did you have in mind?" Erik sidestepped.

Randolph rested the package on the counter. "I bought this segment of a stained-glass window at an auction, and I think it's haunted. Creeps me out. The images in the glass…move."

"Do you have the paperwork?" Erik's past job made him wary of people trying to fence stolen art.

"Right here." Randolph reached into the inside pocket of his coat and withdrew a slightly damp envelope. Inside was the bill of sale from the auction house, along with a detailed description and a photocopied picture of the window itself.

Erik brought Randolph into the break room and spread out the silver-threaded containment mat. He also took a small blanket made from the same blessed and spelled material and set it nearby, as well as grabbing his gloves.

"Can you show me the window?" Erik couldn't help being intrigued. Experience taught him that anything could harbor a ghost or at least soak up negative energy enough to send off uncomfortable vibes. It wasn't uncommon for paintings and old photographs to have a ghostly hitchhiker, but this was the first time he had heard of a haunted window.

Randolph set the box on its side atop the containment mat, and Erik handed him scissors to cut the packing tape that held it shut. He carefully withdrew a two-foot-by-two-foot section of leaded glass.

Ben brought a lamp and they plugged it in. Randolph held the window up against the light, and Erik caught his breath.

"Is that a Tiffany piece?" Erik asked, although he was almost positive it was.

"That's what the seller told me," Randolph said. "I thought I was getting a bargain. I've heard about those windows. Had some in the church where I grew up. I was excited about finally having one of my own. I was going to figure out how to replace one of my regular house windows with it. But then, things went weird."

While Randolph told his story, Erik never took his eyes off the window. Ben moved behind him, where he could also see.

The panel looked like it might have been taken from a larger window. The scene showed two men and a thick old book. It might have been a Bible, but to Erik's eye, it looked more like a grimoire. Tiffany often dealt with religious subjects, but also did windows with flowers, trees, and nature scenes. If this piece had been a custom order, perhaps a book of magic wasn't too strange a request.

Erik would need to run a couple of tests to confirm that the window was indeed a Tiffany. The fame of the creator made copycats and knock-offs brazen and widespread. Even so, previously unknown authentic windows were discovered surprisingly often, hidden away in private homes or small churches.

Still, a first look with a practiced eye suggested that the window was authentic. The dark resonance made him shiver even without touching it to activate his psychometry.

"There!" Ben pointed.

Erik squinted, unsure whether he had really seen motion. Then he saw another shift, slight but unmistakable.

"Did the seller tell you anything else about where the window came from, or who commissioned it?" Erik asked.

Randolph shook his head. "No. He said he bought a numbered lot sight-unseen at an estate sale, and this was in it. I asked why he was selling it, and he said that's what he does—pick through the best stuff in odd lots like that and resells them. Although now I think maybe he knew it was haunted and wanted rid of it."

"What do you want to do with it?" Erik asked.

"I was hoping you'd buy it," Randolph said. "I've heard you're good with spooky stuff."

"I can't resell it if it's haunted, but I can send it to some specialists who can contain it, given its historical value as a Tiffany," Erik told him. "That means I can't pay market value for what a comparable non-haunted Tiffany would be worth. I can give you a couple of hundred dollars, and my thanks for getting a potentially dangerous object out of circulation."

Randolph looked disappointed, but the way he eyed the window like it might bite told Erik that the ghostly phenomenon bothered the man more than he let on. Erik was sorry to let him down if he had hoped for a windfall, and knew that Randolph could still take the window and find another buyer if his ethics didn't stop him from selling it elsewhere without disclosing the problem.

"Take it," Randolph said, shaking his head. "I've had nothing but bad luck since the day I brought it home. I was too afraid to destroy it, but maybe you can before it causes any more problems."

Erik paid cash and wished Randolph well. Ben walked the man to the door and locked up behind him as Erik wrapped the window and its box in the spelled blanket.

"Are you going to read it?" Ben asked.

Erik debated the question, curious to know more about the window. "Not tonight. I'm sure there's a story to go with it, but I'm betting it doesn't have a happy ending. We can tackle that tomorrow, since Alessia and Haley are coming. Maybe one of them will get something from it that I don't."

Erik opened the spelled safe in the back room, where he had placed the *Mohawk* items and the cursed ring. The safe was warded, carved with runes, and made of cast iron with silver medallions inside. It was a protected place to keep potentially dangerous objects until Erik's contact could pick them up and take them to be destroyed or permanently stored in a more secure location.

Once that was done, Erik placed the gloves back under the counter, put the mat away, and dispelled the wards around the table.

"Well, I didn't expect that tonight," he said to Ben.

"Do you think it's a real Tiffany?" Ben asked.

Erik shrugged. "Without doing actual forensic tests, I can't say for sure. But based on my experience, I think so."

"Your experience counts for a lot," Ben replied. Most of Erik's background dealt with revealing frauds or recovering stolen treasures, but Erik had shared stories about pieces that came with a supernatural resonance.

"I've got a lot of questions." Erik took his empty coffee cup to the sink and rinsed it. "That window isn't one that I recognize from the main Tiffany catalogue. Granted, they made thousands of windows, and private commissions might have remained secret, but I'd like to know where the guy who sold it to Peter got it. Tiffanys don't usually show up in the odd lot bin."

"Maybe someone was eager to clean out a house and didn't know what they had," Ben pointed out. "There are whole TV series about that sort of thing."

Most of which Erik scrupulously avoided watching, since they were too close to what he did in the store, with an added dose of breathless hype.

"Those shows work because most of the time, the people who buy up abandoned storage units or the pickers who go to auctions and garage sales are lucky to break even. Finding a missing Picasso painting or a rare first edition book is like winning the lottery," Erik said.

They turned out the lights downstairs, set the security alarm, and headed to the apartment. The rain picked up again, and thunder rumbled in the distance. Erik knew that the window was magically locked down in the safe, and that those spells, in turn, protected them. But he couldn't forget the spooky motion he had seen or the dark energy he sensed, and he vowed to let his contact know as quickly as possible.

"Come on," Ben said, likely sensing Erik's mood. "Let's watch a movie and make popcorn. Perfect for a rainy night. Maybe tomorrow will be boring."

"We should be so lucky," Erik said.

An hour later, the apartment smelled like popcorn, and the action movie's gunfire and explosions rivaled the crash of thunder and the sound of hard rain outside. Erik and Ben sat close together on the couch, enjoying the downtime since they had seen the movie many times.

"You taste good with all that salt and butter." Ben leaned in for a kiss after they finished the popcorn and the movie credits rolled. Ben clicked the remote, turning off the television.

"So do you." Erik returned the kiss and deepened it, adding a sweep of tongue. He loved making out with Ben, whether it led to more or not. After his last disastrous relationship, Erik valued the level of trust between him and Ben, as well as the combustible attraction.

"Ready for bed?" Ben asked as he came up for air. "Because whether we make love or just fall asleep, it'll be better there than on the couch."

"Lead the way." Erik stretched as he rose. His shirt lifted, exposing a strip of skin above his pants, and Ben's gaze heated.

"So sexy," Ben murmured. "Leave the popcorn bucket for tomorrow. I've got other plans for you." He took Erik's hand and led him into their room.

An insistent knock at the door woke them the next morning, long before Alessia and Haley were due to arrive. Erik's phone buzzed, and he saw a message.

Susan: *Cole is trying to reach you about something important.*

"That can't be good." Erik groaned as he swung his legs over the side of the mattress.

"What can't be? And who the hell is knocking?" Ben sounded groggy.

"Cape May's police chief, according to his mother. And it's never a social call."

Erik grabbed a pair of jeans and a T-shirt, ran a hand through his hair, and headed downstairs to find a broad-shouldered man ·in his early thirties at the door. Cole Hendricks looked about as pleased to be there as Erik was to see him.

"Good morning, Chief. What's up?" It wasn't Erik's fault that all of his interactions with the cop involved mobsters and murder. Susan did her best to temper her son's impression of Erik and help Erik see a softer side to the chief. The two men weren't openly hostile, but there was a fair amount of well-deserved skepticism between them.

"Mitchell. Do you know a guy named Peter Randolph?"

Erik stared at him, surprised. He hoped this didn't mean the window had been stolen property. "A man by that name came by the store in the storm last night to sell me a stained-glass window he purchased in an odd-lots sale. I bought it and put it in the safe. It's damaged and can't be resold, so I paid him a finder's fee. Why?"

"He's dead," Hendricks replied. "Murdered. And it has all the hall-marks of a Mob hit."

TWO

BEN

"Murdered?" Ben came downstairs behind Erik and heard Hendricks's announcement. "What happened?"

"May I come in?" Hendricks glanced at Erik, who nodded and stepped aside, shutting the door behind the chief. "We're not putting out details publicly just yet, for a lot of reasons. But someone broke into where he was staying and shot him. Double tap to the back of the head, Mob style."

"Shit," Ben muttered.

"And since you two are the resident Mafia experts in these parts, I thought I'd start with you."

While that might be true, it wasn't something either Ben or Erik wanted to perpetuate. They both came to Cape May for a fresh start, and that included leaving their law enforcement interactions with the Mafia behind them.

Unfortunately, mobsters had long memories.

"We had no reason to connect Peter Randolph with organized crime," Erik told Hendricks. "He had a small stained-glass window that he was in a hurry to sell. All the paperwork was in order, his story of how he got it sounded legitimate and matched the documents, so I made him an offer, and he took it. The window is in the safe."

Hendricks looked at him, and his eyes narrowed as he parsed through what Erik had said.

"Why on earth would he be in such a rush to sell a window that he'd go out in a Godawful thunderstorm at night?" Hendricks asked.

Erik sighed. "Because he was convinced the window was haunted, and it gave him the creeps."

Ben knew from their prior interactions with the chief that Hendricks wasn't inclined to believe in the supernatural. But over the course of solving the crimes that involved him and Erik, ghosts and magic played an important role. Susan also vouched for the reality of Erik's abilities.

"Haunted? How can a window be haunted?"

Erik explained what had happened the previous night and that the window definitely had bad mojo of some sort.

"A Tiffany window? Aren't those the fancy ones in churches? Are you sure it wasn't stolen?" Hendricks asked.

"I saw the paperwork, and based on that and my experience with Interpol busting art thieves, I'm pretty confident that it was a bad bargain on his part," Erik replied. A little frost crept into his tone. Despite trying to stay on good terms with Hendricks, Ben knew that the chief and his partner often butted heads.

"What are you going to do with it—once the investigation is over," Hendricks asked, not quite accusing but definitely all business.

"I'm going to pass it over to a contact of mine who sequesters dangerous objects. Like that warehouse in *Raiders of the Lost Ark*," Erik said.

"I'm being serious."

"So am I," Erik replied. "It'll be kept under specialized security so it can't cause any harm, and probably never see the light of day again."

Hendricks looked surprised, but he recovered quickly. "Why would you buy something just to bury it?"

"Because that's part of what we do at Trinkets, always has been," Erik said. "I'm just carrying on the legacy."

"Seriously? Don't you lose money that way?" Hendricks looked surprised.

Erik shrugged. "It's our mission. Keeping the world a safer place by removing dangerous supernatural objects."

"Huh." Hendricks seemed to consider that for a moment.

"Would mobsters care about the window? Suppose we set aside the 'haunted' stuff. What would something like that be worth?" Hendricks asked. His tone was less challenging than it had been, and Erik wondered whether he was reconsidering his earlier skepticism in light of their shared concern for public safety.

"It depends on the condition and provenance as well as the size," Erik replied. "I didn't examine the window too closely, but it had the hallmarks I'd expect from being old, none of the glass was broken, and the soldering between the pieces was solid. I'm guessing it was done on commission and may have once been part of a larger piece, because the picture wasn't a common theme, so I suspect it came from a collector, not a church or a public building. That said, the price could be thousands of dollars on up."

"Up?"

"A previously unknown piece with a confirmed chain of ownership and commissioned by someone famous could go for a million," Erik replied.

"And Randolph was in such a hurry to get rid of it that he sold it to you for a song instead of cashing in and moving to the islands?" Hendricks asked incredulously.

"Like I said, it creeped him out," Erik said with a shrug.

"Other than the double-tap, is there any link between Randolph and the Mob?" Ben spoke up, hoping to diffuse some of the tension.

"We're working on that," Hendricks replied. "He hasn't been in Cape May long. Got here a few months ago and was renting a room month-to-month at a hotel. Told the manager that he traveled around going to antique and estate sales. The business card he gave her goes to a website that talks about the same thing. No idea yet whether that was a real company or a front."

"Seems like a strange type of guy to get sideways with the Mafia," Ben mused. "Small fish. Murder is messy. If he pissed someone off, they'd be more likely to blow up his car or burn down his office to send a message."

Hendricks rolled his eyes. "You're hip deep in mobsters too. You know, this used to be a quiet little town."

"I've told you everything I know," Erik said. "And whether or not you believe us, we both do our best to leave those old undercover connections behind. There's no inside information. Randolph's murder probably had nothing to do with the window, and it's just a coincidence or a red herring."

"Maybe," Hendricks allowed grudgingly. "But we're going to dig anyhow. Protect the window. At some point, we'll need to see it and enter a photo into evidence."

"Please let us leave it in the safe," Erik said. "That's got special protections for fragile artwork, and we have an excellent security system."

"That's fine, for now. We'll see where the investigation takes us. Just don't take it out of the store until we look into the matter," Hendricks replied. "It stays in Cape May until it's cleared."

Ben saw the way Erik's jaw twitched and knew his partner didn't like the order, but Erik nodded. "It will stay locked up until you give us the okay," he agreed.

"And you probably already knew this, but don't leave town," Hendricks added.

"Darn, and there goes our round-the-world vacation," Ben deadpanned.

"I'll have someone watch the shop, just in case. When I know more, I'll be in touch. Try to keep out of trouble."

"Don't worry. We weren't going anywhere," Erik added. He walked Hendricks out and locked the door behind him, since the shop wasn't open yet.

Erik muttered under his breath. Ben didn't hear the exact words, but the meaning was clear anyway.

"Come on. Let's get showers, dressed, and eat something." Ben herded his partner toward the steps."

He felt vastly better after a shower, especially one that included soap-slicked hand jobs. Erik remained grumpy, but even he had relented a little.

Erik checked his watch. "Alessia and Haley should be here soon."

"I'll make a fresh pot of coffee," Ben volunteered. He couldn't hide his curiosity about working with the newly arrived medium again and hoped she proved to be an ally like Alessia.

"I'm going to get things set up so we're ready when they get here," he told Ben. "And now we can ask if there's magic attached to the haunted window as well."

Before he went to retrieve the *Mohawk* relics he'd found, Erik paused to draw a warded circle around the table and activate its protective magic. He draped the warded cloth over the table and grabbed the special gloves.

Erik headed into the storage room, grateful that all the items were well-marked. Rotating the inventory on display kept the stock fresh for visitors who liked to explore. He found the small box tagged with the items from the computer record, and paused when he put his hand on top.

"Lila, if you're out there and trapped here, maybe we can help you find your way home," he sent silently, although he doubted that the ghost could hear him.

Once he returned to the table and its protections, Erik closed his eyes, trying to pick up on the resonance of the pieces. Strong emotions could remain with an object for a long time, and he suspected that Lila's ill-fated journey could evoke memories.

The images came in a jumble. He glimpsed a ship that he guessed was the *Mohawk*. After that, he saw flames and smoke, then icy water, and the vision ended.

"I saw fragments of memories attached to the items," Erik told Ben when he opened his eyes.

"Let's see what Alessia picks up." Ben glanced at the table. "You decided to leave the stained-glass window in the safe for now?"

Erik nodded. "One problem at a time."

The doorbell rang, and Erik went to check, with Ben close behind. Alessia stood on the front steps. She was in her early forties, with olive skin, black hair, and dark brown eyes. "Come on in. We have a fresh pot of coffee," Erik greeted her

"Good, because I'm not really a morning person," Alessia said.

"How do you take it?" Ben asked.

"Black with sweetener," she replied. "Although I'm not fussy."

"Coming right up," Ben promised. "As you can see, Haley's not here yet."

"She was able to join us?"

"Yeah, but she said she may run late." Erik locked the door and followed Ben and Erik to the table in the break room. Ben noticed that Alessia eyed the salt circle and Erik's other preparations, but didn't seem surprised.

"Expecting trouble?" she asked as Ben went to get her coffee.

"We've learned to be cautious," Erik replied.

Erik and Alessia sat at the table, while Ben stood nearby, ready to lend a hand if needed. "We think bits and pieces from the wreck might be helping to anchor Lila, especially if she worked some kind of hinky protection spell that didn't go as planned."

Ben filled Alessia in on the basics of what they had learned about Lila and the *Mohawk* since their previous conversation. When he finished, Alessia nodded.

"It sounds like we might have a shade instead of a full ghost. Haley could tell you for sure," Alessia said. "That would fit if she was involved with some sort of hedge witch spell that wasn't crafted carefully. Those things can have all sorts of untended consequences. A shade doesn't have the personality or memories of a full ghost, and some people believe that the soul is gone."

"What's left?" Ben asked.

"It's sort of like a photocopy of a picture," Alessia replied. "Faded, even if it's recognizable. There's debate about what kind of energy a shade has if not a soul. Fortunately, we don't have to solve that mystery to be able to break the spell. If not, and the spirit remains, we can have Haley send her on, but I'm thinking we may be able to fix this before she gets here."

Erik wore the silver-threaded gloves as he opened the box,

revealing the cup and saucer with the ship's logo, a salt shaker, and a handful of old buttons.

Alessia closed her eyes and took several deep breaths, letting one hand hover, palm down and open, above the box without touching the pieces. Ben figured she was centering herself.

After a few minutes, she opened her eyes. Her look of concentration shifted to quiet anger.

"That is one of the most tangled-up messes of magic I've ever seen," Alessia said. "Maybe she cobbled it together herself, but if some so-called witch gave it to her or cast it, they were a danger to everyone around them."

"What can you sense?" Ben asked, intrigued but happy to keep a safe distance.

"Good spells are like poems or mathematical equations, in a way," Alessia said. "No extra pieces. Clean, simple, straightforward."

"I'm guessing Lila's spell isn't," Erik said.

"Not even close," Alessia replied. "It reminds me of the sort of nonsense I see in fantasy books where the spell isn't meant to work. She didn't end up bespelling just herself. Somehow it touched everything, but without enough power to actually save her or the ship. This abomination worked just enough to trap her here, but not to actually protect her or anyone else."

"If it touched the whole ship, why aren't there more ghosts?" Ben asked.

"Probably because Lila was the target of the spell. It was likely worded broadly and badly constructed. Sloppy magic makes for unintended consequences," Alessia replied.

Ben felt quite sure that Alessia would have taken measures against the creator of the spell if it hadn't happened so long ago.

"Can you break it?" Erik asked.

"That's the good news. Yes. It's so badly formed I'm surprised it lasted this long," Alessia said.

"Is there anything we can do to help?" Ben asked.

"Stay back from the circle, just in case," she told them. Erik got up from the table and went to stand by Ben. "No matter what I say or do, don't interrupt."

Alessia scrutinized the open box, and then she stretched her hand out again to hover over it. She murmured words Ben didn't catch, and he felt the energy shift in the room. The containment circle flared with a bright golden light and then dimmed. The pieces in the box glowed blood-red and then purple before going dark.

"The air feels…lighter." Ben was unsure of how to put what he sensed into words.

"That's the energy shift of breaking the spell," Alessia replied. "It would have been much stronger without the protective box and the wards."

"Just in case, I'll hand off what's left to my contact in Charleston." Erik still used the gloves as he closed the box.

"No harm in being careful, but the magic is broken," Alessia assured them. "I don't know if Lila was Cape May's only 'woman in white,' but we have one fewer after tonight. And if the souls of the others onboard were affected, that should also release them."

Ben hated to think about being trapped like that, and wrapped his arms around himself to suppress a shiver. Erik laid his hand on Ben's shoulder, grounding and comforting him.

"Can I get you tea or a soda, or something with protein or sugar?" Ben knew how much Erik's psychometry took out of him, and guessed the same might be true for Alessia.

"Yes, please," Alessia replied. "Soda is fine." Ben hurried to bring her a cola and peanut butter crackers. She polished them off quickly.

"Do you need more?" Ben asked. "We've got juice and cookies too."

Alessia shook her head. "I'm okay. I'm just glad it worked, and it looks like we saved Haley the effort."

"Thank you," Erik told her. "When you're up to it, there's another piece in the safe that I would appreciate having you look at. We know it's haunted, but I hadn't really thought about having magic attached too. I want Haley to look at that one as well."

Alessia looked intrigued. "What's the story?"

Erik and Ben took turns filling her in about Peter Randolph.

Considering the tale of a potentially malicious ghost, mobsters, and murder, Alessia seemed to take it in stride.

"Not the worst I've run into," she said. "You really never have a dull day, do you?"

Erik frowned. "I knew when I bought the store that it had a mission as well as a market. It seemed like a good way to use my psychometry to make a difference. At the time, I thought it would be a lot safer than my old job. That part hasn't exactly worked out the way I planned."

Ben could almost see Alessia thinking about their revelations. "I'm not surprised you hit it off with Monty and Haley. This is all their jam."

"We are happy for their help and yours," Erik assured her.

Erik retrieved the haunted window from the safe, still in its protections. He put the box on the table where Alessia still sat within the salt circle. Erik used the silver-threaded gloves to unwrap the window in its box from the protective blanket. He opened the box, but didn't remove the window.

Ben watched as Erik added more salt to the circle around the table for extra protection.

"I only did a superficial reading when the window came in. With you here for backup, I'd like to see if I can get more of a read on it with my psychometry, and then see what magic you pick up," Erik said

"Sounds good," Alessia replied. She closed her eyes and took deep breaths, centering herself. Ben could usually see strong ghosts, but whatever energy tainted the window wasn't something that was visible to him. That didn't stop him from picking up really bad vibes.

They waited, and Ben tried not to fidget.

Erik took off the gloves and let his right hand hover above the window, palm down and fingers splayed. He didn't touch anything. Ben split his attention between watching Erik for any sign of danger or distress and eyeing the window suspiciously in case its image moved.

"It's old…and genuine Tiffany," Erik replied. "I am getting glimpses of the workshop. No idea whether Tiffany himself worked on it. There's a man. I don't know who he is, but there's a dark vibe about him and the book. It's haunted, and I think there's also magic involved."

He paused, frowning. "I'm getting an image of a large stained glass ceiling dome. No context. I don't know whether that's coming from the window's history or its last owner."

Erik suddenly withdrew his hand as if he'd been burned and slammed the box shut.

Alessia's face paled, and she recoiled. She made a gesture of warding. Ben and Erik exchanged a glance, silently agreeing that she had gotten even worse vibes from the window than Erik had. Erik put the gloves back on and hurried to wrap the box in the protective blanket.

"Are you okay?" Ben asked, worried.

Alessia nodded. "Yeah, but that was really dangerous. What did you two pick up from the window?"

"Seriously bad vibes," Ben replied.

"A sense of evil." Erik rejoined them. "I felt like something was reaching for me." Erik had gone pale, and his eyes were wide. Ben knew the energy had to be truly evil to leave Erik shaken. "What did you see?" he asked Alessia.

"I'm not a medium, but I'm fairly certain it's possessed by a malicious ghost," Alessia said, seeming to slowly be regaining equanimity. "It's not spelled, of that I'm certain, but it does carry a strong resonance of magic. I don't know whether it's the man you saw in the image or the prior owner or someone else, but I don't think that can be cleansed by anything short of an exorcism, and maybe not even then. When Haley arrives, you can ask her, but I'm afraid that one may be too much even for her."

Erik nodded. "Thank you. I suspected as much, but it's good to verify. I didn't buy it for resale. I bought it to pass off to an organization that will permanently store it on magical lockdown so it can't ever hurt anyone again."

Ben went to the fridge and came back with small bottles of orange juice for Alessia and Erik, which they accepted gratefully and knocked back like whiskey.

"I'm sorry about that," Erik said after they had a few moments to collect themselves.

Ben went to answer a knock at the door and returned with Haley.

"Hey, everyone," Haley greeted them. "Did you start the party without me?"

Erik shook his head. "A little, Alessia cleared a bad spell, so it was out of the way before you arrived, and we just read a new acquisition and confirmed it had seriously bad mojo. You can look at the other piece as well, but I'd rather not put you in danger."

"Trust me on this one, Haley, leave it for someone else," Alessia said.

"Okay then." Haley seemed to accept Alessia's advice without another thought. "You said there's a ghost you wanted me to contact?" Haley poured herself a cup of coffee and sat at the table next to Alessia.

"Yes, if you can reach him," Erik said.

"Tell me what you need, and I'll make the connection if I can," Haley replied.

"Peter Randolph sold the window to me and then got shot. I know the cops won't accept ghost testimony, but I'd like to see if Randolph knew his attacker," Erik answered.

Haley set her coffee aside and then rubbed the palms of her hands together. "Okay. Let's do this. But considering the source, I'm not going to channel the spirit, I'll just relay what he tells me." She paused for a few deep breaths and then opened her eyes.

"Peter Randolph, we want to solve your murder and bring the killers to justice," Haley said. "Please appear to us."

Another silent moment passed, and then Randolph's ghost took shape, looking like he had when he had shown up on their doorstep. To Ben's relief, the revenant didn't appear bearing his death wound. Ben had seen enough head shots to last a lifetime.

"Not the window," Haley repeated the ghost's words.

"You were killed for another reason that isn't related to the window you sold me?" Erik asked.

"There's another ghost," Haley told them. "I don't recognize him. The second man says they want the dome. It's priceless and powerful."

"What dome?" Ben and Erik spoke in unison. Ben wondered if it was the same stained-glass dome that had shown up in Erik's vision.

"From a hotel. The second man was the auctioneer, and he believes he was murdered because the killers thought he knew where it went; he didn't. Randolph said he didn't either," Haley repeated their comments.

"Was the dome stolen?" Ben asked.

Haley paused. "It disappeared in the last days of the liquidation sale. The second ghost said there was a lot of chaos. So many big boxes and trucks coming and going. It was packed into several large crates, but he thinks someone must have slipped them out without showing papers."

"Had someone bought the dome?" Erik asked.

"A single bidder paid several million dollars for it. But afterward, when they tried to track down the buyer's information, it was all phony. They paid with a suitcase full of cash," Haley said.

"Nothing suspicious about that at all," Ben remarked.

"He thinks that his killer either worked for the mystery bidder or wanted to find the dome to steal it from the buyer. Randolph said his killer kept asking him where the dome was and didn't believe him when he said he didn't know," Haley recounted.

"Does the auctioneer know who killed him?" Ben asked.

"He doesn't know his name, but he saw him at the auction."

Erik and Ben exchanged a look. Ben's computer pinged, and he ignored it for the moment.

"Collectors have long memories, and they can be patient," Haley repeated what Randolph's spirit answered. "Maybe the killer has been watching him all these years and waiting for him to lead them to the dome."

Strain showed in Haley's face, and Ben knew she would have to release the link to the ghosts soon.

"Thank you for your help," Haley told the ghosts. "I can help you pass over, if you want." She listened intently to a conversation Ben couldn't hear. Erik shook his head to let Ben know he didn't hear the ghosts, either.

"Then go in peace. This conversation is over." She murmured what sounded to Ben like a banishing spell.

"What did he say there at the end?" Erik asked.

"He didn't want to pass on yet. Said he wanted to see the 'sons of bitches who killed me' get what was coming to them," Haley replied.

"Guess I can't blame him for that." Ben brought the pot of coffee to refill their cups.

"Thank you for trusting me," Haley said after she had another cup and looked more settled. "I'm happy to be your ghost connection whenever I can be of help." She grinned. "I feel like I'm part of a secret club that protects the community."

"You're not far off," Ben replied. "Thank you both."

"We truly appreciate your help," Erik added. They walked Haley and Alessia to the door and promised to get together for dinner sometime without haunted artifacts or dangerous ghosts.

"That went well," Erik said as they returned to the kitchen.

"Do you think we traumatized Alessia?" Ben asked, only partly joking.

Erik shook his head. "Doubtful. She seems to have a good bit of experience dealing with the dark side. Her reaction and comments made me doubly glad we kept the window in the safe. I don't think the cops are prepared for that."

"I want to know what dome Randolph was talking about," Ben said. "I got the feeling it could be really important."

"More research," Erik replied. He checked the time. "Susan will be here any minute. I'm going to sweep up the salt and get ready to open the store."

"I'll see if Randolph's name comes up on my private investigator databases," Ben replied. While he no longer took new clients, he had found that having access to those resources came in handy, given how their past lives had followed them. "And I'll see if there are any reports of stolen Tiffany windows."

Erik nodded. "It's off-season, so I'm not expecting to be swamped with customers. Susan can handle them. I thought I'd sniff around on the discussion boards for museums and art investigators and see if there have been new windows found or thefts reported. It's a long shot, but worth it. I might even find something about a dome."

"Are you gonna tell Hendricks what Haley and Alessia told us?" Ben teased.

"Only if he stops being a dick." Erik swallowed the last of his coffee. The way his throat bobbed gave Ben all kinds of X-rated thoughts, which would have to wait until later.

"He's just doing his job," Ben said aloud what they both knew. "He didn't haul us into the station for a statement or try to take the window. He could have been a bigger pain."

"I know," Erik admitted. "Still doesn't mean I like the attitude."

"Think of it this way, he's trying to save face. It's hard to be the top dog sheriff when we bring Bratva and the Newark Mob to his doorstep."

"Yeah, yeah. I get it. It could be worse," Erik said.

"And Susan goes to bat for us behind the scenes," Ben reminded him. "I imagine he feels ganged up on."

"Good." Erik poured a fresh cup of coffee. "Okay. Come get me if you need me." He kissed Ben and headed for the store.

Ben refilled his mug and checked in with Jenny, his administrative assistant, to make sure he wasn't needed at the office. After a quick run through email, he logged into the specialized resources available because he kept his investigator license current.

Peter Randolph was a common enough name that it took him a while to filter his search. That returned a reasonably sized list of possibilities, and Ben started working his way through them.

Television shows made private investigators look like glamorous action heroes. The truth was, they knew how to use research tools, databases, public records, and an acute insight into human behavior to cut through lies and distractions. It helped to be a stubborn bastard. The action part was Ben's least favorite, since shootouts and fistfights were a good way to get killed.

Ben liked the challenge of research and approached it like a puzzle or a game. The first hour flew by, and he filled a sheet of paper with notes as he went from site to site. Once he had whittled down some of the possibilities, Ben intended to contact friends in the business who might have more insight. Little by little, he'd unravel the mystery.

In the background, he heard the bell on the door downstairs as it opened and closed, and knew Susan had arrived. He figured Erik would get an earful. Susan wouldn't betray confidences from either Erik or her son, the sheriff, but she did her best to make sure the men got along and worked together.

"How's it going?"

Erik's voice startled Ben, and he nearly sloshed his coffee. He glanced at the time and realized most of the morning had slipped by.

"Slow progress. The way it always goes." Ben pointed to the monitor with his pencil. "I can't trace the stained-glass window with Randolph's credit card, so I'm guessing he paid cash."

"That's pretty normal for auctions and odd lot sales," Erik said. "Some of those places don't even like checks."

Ben nodded. "That's what I figured. I looked for the notices of sales like that in the past two weeks within a hundred-mile radius of Cape May. Hell of a lot of them, but probably fewer than in high summer."

"And?"

"I found a sale run by Otis Jones. His whole business is auctions, estate liquidations, and closeouts. He had a long list of things that were in the sale—no pictures—and listed a stained-glass panel," Ben said. "So, I called him."

"Was he the right guy? Did he sell the window to Randolph?" Erik asked.

Ben nodded. "Yeah. He remembered it. Thought it was pretty, but in his words: 'creepy as fuck.' Got it from an estate sale of a guy out in

Wildwood who died in his nineties with no family. He mentioned off-handedly that the local gossips thought the old man was a mobster."

Erik barked a laugh. "Figures."

"Doesn't it? Anyhow, Jones said that Randolph spotted the window right away. Jones couldn't confirm that it was a real Tiffany, so he couldn't charge top dollar, but Randolph was still willing to pay two thousand dollars for it. Jones didn't like the window, so he didn't haggle."

"Someone else who gives up more money to be rid of it," Erik noted.

"Uh-huh. Plus an organized crime connection. But if someone from the old guy's past wanted the window, why didn't they go to the sale? Or steal it before the event even happened?" Ben replied.

"Did you get the name of the old man? Maybe we can find a connection that will make sense of this," Erik suggested.

"I'm on it. Given the Wildwood connection, he's more likely to be Newark Mob or Atlantic City than Bratva," Ben said. "Be thankful for small favors."

Ben's computer pinged, and he leaned forward. "Got a hit on Randolph." He scanned the information and looked up.

"Interesting. Thirty years ago, Randolph's business partner, a guy named John Bellamy, was also murdered. The police noted 'suspected organized crime violence' but never found the killer. They owned a salvage and liquidation company that was one of several involved in selling off the assets of the Commodore Wilson Hotel before it was demolished."

Ben and Erik stared at each other for a moment as the importance of that tidbit sank in.

"Holy shit. I swear that damn hotel is a vampire. It keeps coming back from the dead," Erik muttered.

The Commodore Wilson had once been the crown jewel of Cape May and, in its day, the largest hotel in the world. The huge luxury property commanded a beach view and offered lodging, meeting services, and food that drew loyal visitors who returned year after year.

Over the hotel's long life, it had a checkered past, ruining everyone who owned it, whether they were hoteliers, fire-breathing evangelists, or sketchy self-improvement gurus. Rumors circulated from the earliest days of Mafia money behind the scenes. Despite a turn as a fundamentalist Christian retreat center, gossip blamed the bad luck on cursed magic and deals with the devil. Ben and Erik believed the land itself was a dark genius loci, quintessentially evil.

After the Commodore Wilson fell into receivership and disrepair for the last time, no one rushed in to save the aging property. It was stripped of any saleable assets or décor, which were sold in a massive auction, and then imploded. In the thirty years since then, the property had been home to a variety of businesses, none of which prospered.

"Okay, this is a long shot, but hear me out," Ben said.

"I'm used to your crazy, so hit me up."

Ben gave him the side-eye. "You said you thought that the book in the stained-glass panel was a grimoire. What if the old guy who owned the window was a *strega*, a Mob witch? Maybe he worked for the Mafia families who owned the Commodore Wilson property over the years to blunt the curse of the land as best he could."

"It's certainly possible," Erik mused. "But why come after Randolph now? The panel he brought in didn't have a connection to the Commodore Wilson. And even if it did, the hotel was blown up thirty years ago. There's something here we're missing."

Ben sat back in his chair and twiddled his pencil. "That's what I've got. What made you come looking for me?"

"Oh, that. I always thought of Tiffany windows being in churches and mansions. But it turns out, there's a dark side," Erik said. "A Tiffany window could either have been created by Louis Comfort Tiffany himself, or later on, by artisans at the Tiffany Company working under his guidance. According to what I found, there were at least twenty Tiffany windows made celebrating the Confederacy, both in Richmond, Virginia, and elsewhere in the Confederate states. They were put in churches and universities."

"No shit," Ben said, eyes widening. "Wait. Wasn't Cape May part of the Underground Railroad, getting slaves out of the South?"

Erik nodded. "Yep. That's why the Harriet Tubman Museum is here. Interestingly enough, both well-to-do abolitionists and slave owners liked Cape May, at least before the Civil War."

"Tiffany didn't care who bought their windows?" Ben replied.

"Apparently not," Erik agreed with a disgusted twitch of his lip. "They did a lot of commissions for homes, mausoleums, and private chapels. Either they intentionally destroyed records to ensure privacy, or they were 'lost' over the years, but it's not uncommon for previously unknown Tiffanys to show up even now. Collectors love finding a hidden gem, and the lack of publicity makes the purchase desirable for people with lots of money and something to hide."

"Like mobsters," Ben said.

"Yeah. Why does everything always come back to that?"

"Just our luck." Ben paused. "Mausoleums? Really? Pretty fancy for a place hardly anyone will ever see."

Erik shrugged. "Maybe it didn't seem extravagant to someone with a lot of money or guilt."

"Not something I'm ever likely to know about," Ben replied. "Do you think anyone is going to come after the window?"

Erik grimaced. "I hope not. The property and building are heavily warded and so is the safe. If you didn't notice with the storm, there was a police car outside last night, and I'm guessing it will be there again tonight. I think there's been a plainclothes officer stationed nearby all day. Hendricks said he'd have someone watching. I'd just send the damned window to the folks in Charleston to get rid of, but Hendricks said we couldn't."

"Any news from Susan?" Ben switched subjects.

"Plenty about the Awesome Autumn Festival, but nothing else," Erik replied. "They want more ghost stories, so we're supposed to weave that in. And stuff about pirates, if it applies."

Cape May was said to be one of the most haunted towns on the East Coast, and had once been a haven for pirates, so both fit with the darker side of a resort otherwise known for its chill vibe.

"I saw the email. Monty's going to have his hands full with all the events around the lighthouse and the concrete ship and the watch tower," Ben said. "I know the festival is for a good cause and raises a lot of money for charity, but it's a lot of work for everyone."

"I also asked Susan to take a couple of days off because of the creepy window thing. If someone does try to steal it or attack us, I don't want her to become a target."

"Good idea. I'm surprised Hendricks hadn't already lobbied her to stay home," Ben replied.

Erik chuckled. "Maybe he did, but Susan definitely makes up her own mind about these things."

"I'm hoping nothing will happen, but I'm glad she'll be safe," Ben agreed.

"We've only got a couple of hours until closing time," Erik said. "I'm curious to see if anyone suspicious comes in. It's a shame Hendricks can't accept evidence from ghosts. Not that he'd believe us anyhow."

To Ben's relief, the rest of the day passed quietly. He continued his research into the dead men's criminal history, and Erik did a deep dive into the lore of Tiffany windows on his computer downstairs.

"Here." Ben handed Erik a small bottle of orange juice and a candy bar. "You look like roadkill."

"You say the nicest things." Erik accepted the snacks gratefully. "Doing the read on the window took a lot out of me. I'm impressed that Alessia held up so well."

"I'm leaning into the theory that the book is a grimoire and the man was a witch," Erik added. "Putting the box back into the safe was like closing a door. The dark vibes shut off immediately."

"Good. Leave it there until we can get help," Ben replied. "I think we're going to need a team for this. At least we know a little more than when we started."

"Answers and more questions," Erik said. "Like always."

Ben went to check his computer when it pinged. "Got a few more hits," he reported.

"Anything good?"

Ben paused to read through the notices. "The old guy who was the Wildwood collector was Grant Samuels. Thanks to money, lawyers, and friends in high places, he doesn't have a criminal record, but there are notes about his questionable associates," Ben said. "No one comes right out and calls him a witch, but the comments mention that he had exceptional people skills and seemed able to overcome any opposition."

"Right. That means he either used magic or killed people who posed a problem. Maybe both," Erik interpreted the deliberately vague description.

"That's what I get out of it," Ben agreed. "For Reynolds and Bellamy, it's a different story. 'Known Mafia associates' shows up in both their records. They've got a history with shady auction houses that might be fronts for organized crime. After all, it's a largely cash business."

"Sounds like the Mob's kind of thing," Erik said. "Anything else?"

"They both had arrests on suspicion of money laundering, but the charges were dropped," Ben read aloud. "Otherwise, they're clean, not even parking tickets."

"If they were useful to someone in the Mafia, getting charges dropped isn't hard," Erik remarked. "I'm guessing that some of the town's prior police chiefs weren't as upstanding as Chief Hendricks."

Ben shrugged. "That might explain why he's such a tight-ass. Trying to make sure no one thinks he's cut from the same cloth."

"We both know Susan would whip his butt," Erik replied with a laugh.

Ben glanced at his watch. "I think we've done enough for one day." He closed down his laptop. "Tomorrow, I want to see what else I can dig up on who some of those 'known Mafia associates' were and see if that leads anywhere."

"I need to look into this mysterious Tiffany dome and see what I can come up with," Erik agreed. "Something that significant must have sparked interest from the art world as well as the press. It would have been a large installation. Maybe I can get an idea of who might have been unusually interested in it."

Ben rose from the table. "How about we make some nachos and watch another movie? Then I'll suck your brains out your dick and you won't worry about mobsters anymore tonight."

"Promise? I'll return the favor," Erik teased.

"Cross my heart," Ben replied with a lascivious grin.

THREE

ERIK

"Forecast says more storms coming in," Erik announced when he came up from the store to check in with Ben after breakfast the next morning.

"Figures. The comment boards are jumping with people swearing they've seen strange things." Ben pushed away from the table and stretched. "No woman in white. We might have taken care of Lila. But the latest is the ghost train on those tracks where the sand washed away."

For nearly eighty years, the beach covered a stretch of private railroad tracks that once carried train cars full of sand taken elsewhere for industrial use. Erosion exposed the iron rails and wooden crossbars that everyone had forgotten about, resurrecting its ghosts in the process.

"If I remember right, that was never a passenger line," Erik replied.

Ben nodded. "Crazy that they thought it was okay to take sand away from a beach, but that was back in the twenties and thirties. During the Second World War, the government used the tracks in their munitions testing. The tracks still appear and disappear in the sand depending on the tides and erosion. But right now, the storms have exposed them, and that brought back the ghosts as well."

"Did you figure out the backstory on the ghosts?" Erik asked.

"There's not much to go on, but what I could find suggests they're probably workers from the sand company who got killed on the job. That squares with what people are posting on social media, about seeing ghostly men in bloody worker's clothing near the tracks." Ben looked up from his screen.

"There was another large magnesite mining operation that ran during World War II, and ended up being a Superfund site for pollution," Ben added. "Any big operation like that usually has some worker deaths from machinery or getting sick from the conditions."

"We should be able to check with Monty and Jon about the tracks, since they're always at the beach," Erik replied. "Anything else?"

"A couple of urban explorers posted about ghosts where the old World War I camp used to be," Ben told him. "There's not much left of the original Camp Wissahickon except some abandoned concrete bunkers. Everything else is overgrown. They went legend tripping to check out the bunkers and ran into some children's spirits and ghosts in military uniforms that the explorers claim ran them off."

"Huh. Kids?"

"Yeah. I found this." Ben pointed to his screen. "Before the government built the camp, there used to be an amusement park on that property with a skating rink, a stage, and a few rides. They repurposed all that, and later on, most of the original buildings burned down. There's still an active Coast Guard Training Center on some of the same land."

"You think the children's ghosts were probably from the amusement park?"

"That's my guess. Those old-time rides weren't just scary, they were actually dangerous."

"Any military ghosts?" Erik asked.

"Not as many as I'd have expected," Ben replied. "But a few."

"I don't remember hearing about active ghosts or problems at those locations," Erik said.

"We haven't. I'm blaming the storms. Plenty of legends say that all that energy in the atmosphere rouses ghosts," Ben said.

Erik started to pace. "Okay, so right now there's no situation we need to fix with the weird tracks, and the ghosts at the bunker and military camp aren't hurting anyone. That's good, but it could change depending on how the spirits react to the storm energy."

"We can't be everywhere at once," Ben pointed out. "We'll keep looking for reports, decide what needs action, and go from there. We can get help if we need it from Haley, Monty, or Alessia."

"I've been digging up more on Tiffany domes." Erik turned a chair around and straddled it to face Ben. "There's a huge one in Chicago at a museum. The others I've found are in hotels or public buildings. I also turned up a lot of references to the dome at the Commodore Wilson. It was a popular place over the years for wedding ceremonies and photos, and in the years that the hotel was run by a fire-breathing minister, he gave sermons under the dome."

"Interesting," Ben replied. "I imagine it shows up in a lot of people's vacation pictures, from when the Commodore Wilson was a ritzy resort."

"That, too. But so far, I haven't found much about the dome's background except that it was there from the opening day, and considered an artistic gem," Erik said. "But I think maybe there's some dark magic—or at least bad luck—that goes along with certain Tiffany windows."

"Oh, yeah?" Ben sipped his coffee.

"Some of the smaller panels Tiffany made for other locations got stolen. People fought over privately commissioned pieces during divorces or inheritance squabbles," Erik replied. "A couple of owners were murdered, and a few owners just disappeared, with or without their windows."

"If they were mobsters or corrupt robber baron types, they might have had it coming, and the windows didn't actually cause the bad luck," Ben pointed out. "There's a pretty small sliver of the population who can afford Tiffany windows, and most didn't earn their money by being saints."

"I'm well aware," Erik replied in a dry tone, thinking back to all the high-profile fraud and theft cases he had handled when he put his art knowledge to work for Interpol. "Famous artwork is different from owning an expensive car or building a mansion. There might be other Tiffany windows, but there's only one of any given type. Like paintings. There are other Picassos, but only one *Guernica*."

"I always thought the attraction was getting to display the famous art and show it off," Ben remarked. "Kinda like 'nah-nah-nah, I have this and you don't.'"

Erik chuckled at Ben's phrasing. "There's definitely some of that, depending on the person. Some collectors want to show off their wealth and be admired, or spark jealousy. Or if they donate the money for a piece to be installed at a museum or church, they want credit for using their wealth for a good outcome."

He sighed. "But there are others who cause problems. They want to possess the art, and they don't want to share it with anyone, even letting people view it. They're super rich and very paranoid, sometimes with good reason if they're mobsters or corrupt politicians, or if they stole the piece."

Ben looked puzzled. "So let me get this right—there are filthy rich guys out there who will drop a shit ton of money on a famous piece of art, then hide it so it's never seen again?"

"There's a long list of famous artwork that just disappeared," Erik replied. "Stolen, destroyed in fires, or lost, like the pieces that went down with the Titanic. Odds are good that the ones that were stolen or just vanished without verified destruction are hidden away somewhere."

"Which kept you busy, back in your old job," Ben observed.

"We chased the leads we got on art theft; and had to authenticate paintings that mysteriously turned up and were actually frauds. But we didn't have the staff to find them all. There's a lot out there that probably won't show up until old men die and their heirs get into a fight over the spoils," Erik added.

"I can almost understand not sharing something that special with other people," Ben mused. "But I'd still want to be able to go in my secret room and sit there and look at my stolen artwork. Something like the Commodore Wilson's stained-glass dome isn't doing anyone any good in a box. It would have to be installed so the light could go through. Right?"

"I imagine someone with enough money to buy it could arrange for a discreet installation that wouldn't be visible from outside," Erik said. "Like the Amber Room."

"Haven't heard about that one," Ben admitted.

"Imagine a whole room paneled with amber in the Catherine Palace in St. Petersburg before World War II," Erik replied. "It was disassembled by the Nazis, and no one's seen it since. Some people think it was stored in a location that got bombed, but most of us in the business believe there's an oligarch out there who has it hidden away."

"Seems like that would be a hard secret to keep."

"Some of the most notorious collectors are immortal," Erik said, and saw the surprise register on Ben's face.

"Think about it. They have money, connections, and plenty of time. They can assure their retainers' loyalty. Some of them are actual connoisseurs, while I've always thought others want to be surrounded by things that remind them of their mortal life," Erik added.

"I guess that makes sense," Ben replied. "Although it certainly complicates recovering the items."

"Definitely true." Erik knew Ben had heard him in the throes of nightmares remembering the times his old job had nearly gotten him killed. Ben's past as a cop and detective kept him up plenty of nights as well.

"How do you want to play this, assuming we actually get a lead on the whereabouts of the dome?" Ben asked.

Erik thought for a moment. "If the dome or the owner is still in Cape May, then we call in reinforcements, if necessary, and intervene. If it's left the area, it's no longer our problem. We can pass the word along to Cassidy, Sorren, and our other contacts, but I got out of chasing down stolen art for a reason." He smiled and reached out to touch Ben's cheek. "And you've given me another very good reason to stay safe."

Ben pressed his lips to Erik's for a kiss that made silent promises. "I'll take a rain check on that." his voice into a sexy growl.

"I'll hold you to that."

Ben turned back to his screen. "I did find something else about the bunkers and the old military camp, and I wanted to bounce it off you."

"Shoot," Erik said.

"This was on one of the conspiracy boards, so factor that in," Ben warned. Although they often got legitimate tips about supernatural goings-on from chat groups and legend tripper sources, sorting out the real information from the tall tales took time and knowledge.

"Sometimes those pay off," Erik admitted. "Find something legit?"

"Maybe," Ben replied. "I found a post about a soldier who was supposed to marry the love of his life, but he was killed in a munitions explosion."

"Sounds possible, but not really our thing," Erik said.

"The story also said that the explosion happened because someone targeted the base and bunker with bad magic," Ben added. "As in, a dark witch attacked the military base and tried to blow it up."

Erik frowned. "Why? What was in it for the witch? And how would the person telling the story know that?"

"All good questions," Ben admitted. "I don't have answers. But it raises a magical element that seems to fit with all the recent unusual ghost sightings. If the big storms are wreaking havoc with the energy, it's probably juicing up the spirits. We've been lucky that so far; they've just been more visible. But what happens when the ghost is angry and wants revenge? That could cause some big problems."

"Especially if things don't settle down by the time the festival gets into full swing," Erik replied. "And after the autumn festival, there's Halloween, then Thanksgiving, Christmas, and New Year's, and they all have lots of special events. Right now, Cape May is about as quiet as it gets until January."

"It would be good if we didn't have ghosts and mobsters causing trouble," Ben concluded. "Hey, no pressure, right?"

"Yeah, right. Tomorrow, let's go see Monty and get his read on the ghost problem," Erik suggested. "I'll close the store since Susan is still taking time off. With luck, if there are mobsters watching us, they're less likely to jump us in broad daylight."

"But not impossible."

"No, but I think they'll bide their time until they think we know something valuable," Erik said. "And I wouldn't put it past Hendricks to keep the plainclothes tail on us, just in case. Not sure how I feel about it, but maybe it'll come in handy."

"We should probably ask Monty about those ghost tracks as well," Ben said.

"And there's something I want to see at the cemetery," Erik added. "I found out where Grant Samuels, the Wildwood collector who sold the haunted window, is buried. Turns out he owned a carved stone angel created by Tiffany back in the 1930s, and had a headstone commissioned more recently that holds to the designs that the real Tiffany studio used back in the day."

Ben looked at him. "The same Tiffany that did windows also made tombstones?"

"Yep. There are even some at Arlington National Cemetery," Erik replied. "The company did hundreds of them before the original firm closed in the 1930s. Very Art Deco. The designers like lilies."

"What do you think we might find at Samuel's gravesite?" Ben asked.

"Dunno. Just a hunch. Might be nothing; but might as well do a side quest while we're out."

Ben chuckled at the gaming reference. "Works for me. This afternoon, I think we should call Cassidy and Sorren and fill them in on the haunted window," Ben said. "Even if we can't get the glass to them right away, they can be making arrangements to pass it on to their safehouse."

"I agree," Erik said. "And we can run some of the other names by them as well. I'm sure they have a whole different set of sources than what we can run through the databases."

"Until we're ready for that call, I'm going to keep researching," Ben said. "With the bad weather, there haven't been immediate requests for showing rental properties, and this is the slow time of the year for new tenants. Jenny has the office covered until things pick up. I'm hoping that by the time the storms ease off, we'll have dealt with the ghost problem and kept the mobsters at bay."

"We can hope," Erik agreed. "I'm catching up on paperwork, since no one's stopping in to buy."

———

After sundown, Erik closed the shop early and settled in at the table with Ben for their call to Cassidy.

"I texted earlier to make sure now would be a good time," he told Ben. "It's dark outside, so Sorren can join us."

Cassidy Kincaide picked up on the first ring. "Hi Erik and Ben. I've got Sorren with me as well as Teag and Rowan. I'm hoping that one of us can help you with your questions."

Cassidy owned Trifles and Folly, an antique and curio shop in Charleston, much like the store Erik had bought. He discovered after the purchase that his store and Cassidy's had an intertwined history, and worked with coalitions like the Alliance and the Briggs Society that united mortals and immortals in getting rid of cursed or dangerously haunted objects and stopping supernatural threats.

Like Erik, Cassidy was a psychometric. Teag's weaver witch magic enabled him to weave spells and protections into cloth. Rowan was a powerful witch as well. Sorren was a 600-year-old vampire who had helped Cassidy's ancestors found the store several hundred years ago and also helped to found Trinkets.

"We've got two issues, and while I don't think they're related, I'm not ruling it out," Erik said. "The severe thunderstorms we're getting seem to have energized ghosts that aren't usually problems, and I'm afraid that if it keeps up, some of them will turn violent. We've also got a haunted Tiffany window that's gotten its prior owners murdered by the Mob, and a missing Tiffany stained-glass dome that's attracting the wrong kind of attention."

"You guys never do anything by halves," Cassidy said. "Wow. Where do you want to start?"

Erik and Ben took turns describing the ghost incidents they had handled, as well as what they had learned from Haley, Monty, and Jon.

"If the storm energy is just making the ghosts more visible for a while, that's one thing," Ben said, "but we're worried about it feeding into anger and vengeance and becoming a danger. We're working with the local coven and a couple of mediums, but Cape May has a lot of ghosts if they all decide to go psycho at once."

Cassidy chuckled. "Being from Charleston, I understand. We have a pretty high ghost-to-living people ratio too. How much longer is the bad weather supposed to last?"

"None of the weather people agree," Erik chimed in. "This is always storm season, and it varies year to year, but we've got a pretty severe streak predicted. I don't know if the ghosts will steadily gain energy as the storms get more powerful, but that could become a problem."

"Most of the spirits aren't going to be strong enough to channel energy like that," Rowan told them. "For the weaker ghosts who haven't retained a clear sense of self, they aren't likely to gain more abilities than just becoming more visible."

"We get enough hurricanes here in Charleston, we've had experience with the problem," Cassidy added.

"You're right to be concerned about the more sentient spirits," Rowan continued. "Fortunately, not every ghost wants to go vengeful. They might use the energy boost to try to cross over for good. But the few who have a lot of unresolved issues or died traumatically definitely could become dangerous. I can send your friendly neighborhood witch variations on protection spells, as well as some of the banishments and exorcisms for the mediums if you want."

"Yes, please," Erik said. "I'd feel better having a few more tools at hand."

"Check your email," Rowan said. "Glad to help."

"Now what about the Tiffany windows?" Teag asked. "Those don't just turn up every day. We've had a few over the years at Trifles and Folly, but they weren't haunted."

Once again, Erik and Ben tag-teamed filling the others in on what they had discovered. "The haunted window was a commissioned piece, which makes it more valuable because it's one-of-a-kind," Erik told them. "The dome from the Commodore Wilson hotel was huge, famous, and priceless. Something like that doesn't just disappear without powerful people involved."

"We're afraid that in addition to being rich, powerful, and mobbed up, the collector who stole the dome might be immortal," Ben added.

The call fell silent for a few seconds. "That's possible," Sorren said finally. "It would take a great deal of wealth—or magic—to hide such a treasure unless it was kept boxed up. A true collector would want it on display, even if he was the only one to see it. If it vanished thirty years ago, that's still well within the lifespan of a mortal, perhaps a powerful witch."

"Two people have died because of the smaller haunted window," Erik pointed out. "The cops don't want us to move it from our safe, but I'm not going to rest easy until we've handed it off to the Alliance or the Briggs Society for permanent resolution."

"I think we're both worried that the haunted window showing up may have gotten the attention of the person who stole the Tiffany dome," Ben said. "Or brought a would-be obsessed collector out of hiding."

"When you are able to move the haunted window, we'll send resources to take it off your hands," Sorren assured them.

"My kind tend to be solitary types," Sorren replied. "Contrary to what you see on television, we don't hang out in private nightclubs together. There's not a lot of trust unless the other person has been known for a long time, and even then, sadly, betrayals happen. Immortality doesn't necessarily bring out the best in people."

"Neither does great wealth," Erik remarked. "Put that together with magic and it doesn't bode well."

He knew that Sorren wasn't the only vampire who intervened on behalf of mortals and saw themselves as protectors. Erik was also well aware that Sorren and his like-minded companions were not typical.

"I will make quiet inquiries about the Tiffany dome," Sorren said. "I assume you think it's somehow tied in with the smaller window?"

"The dome was part of the Commodore Wilson since it was built," Erik replied. "The land is an evil genius loci, and everything about the hotel was snake-bit. All the owners went broke and had horrible misfortune. Such a huge, expensive, one-of-a-kind piece like the dome seems likely to have absorbed some of that bad juju. At best, it's unlucky, at worst, it's cursed. But since we don't know where it is or who controls it, we don't know if it's dangerous."

"I'll see what I can find out," Sorren replied. "Although trying to reclaim it is inadvisable for a host of reasons, especially if we're dealing with a vampire Mob witch."

Erik flinched at the description, since it put his worst fear about the missing dome into words. "Not planning any rescue missions," he assured them. "Just want to know what we're dealing with, and who we might be up against."

"I'll see what I can find out through our channels as well," Cassidy said, and Erik could hear Teag and Rowan murmur in agreement. "We'll let you know what we find out."

"Thank you." Erik felt some of his stress subside. "We might be overthinking this, but just in case, it's good to have options."

"Absolutely," Cassidy agreed. "We'll be back in touch as soon as we've got news. In the meantime, be careful."

They ended the call, and Ben closed his laptop. "We didn't exactly get answers, but I feel better knowing that they're going to help look into things."

"I hope I'm worrying too much, but my intuition says I'm not," Erik confessed.

Ben reached out to take his hand. "I made a cottage pie this afternoon. We can have a quiet dinner at home and make an early evening of it." He gave Erik a lascivious grin. "I can think of some ways to get you tired enough to sleep."

"I like the way you think." Erik leaned in to kiss him. "I still don't know how I got lucky enough to get you."

"We both got lucky," Ben pointed out, rising to turn on the oven. "And tonight, we can get even luckier."

They kept conversation light over dinner, and Erik found that despite the tension of the last few days, it hadn't affected his appetite. Afterward, they watched some feel-good home and garden shows before heading to bed earlier than usual.

"How do you want it?" Ben slipped beneath the covers naked and held him close.

"I don't care, as long as I feel you," Erik admitted. "I don't want to think about anything, just feel."

"I can make that happen." Ben leaned in to start with gentle kisses that became more intense as they roamed from Erik's lips to his neck, down his torso, and then to his thighs and groin.

Erik groaned, and Ben licked the sensitive skin and lightly nipped, getting a shimmy of hips in response. Ben knew exactly how to make Erik's brain turn off, silencing his thoughts as his body's pleasure took priority.

Ben swirled his tongue around Erik's stiff cock, then flicked the tip up and down the shaft before returning to the sensitive head. He slicked the fingers of his other hand and began to roll Erik's balls and toy with his hole as Ben's mouth worked his cock.

"So good," Erik groaned, earning him a dirty chuckle from Ben in response.

Ben took his time, while Erik hungered for release. His hips bucked, and his hands clenched the sheets.

"Please, make me come," Erik begged.

Ben teased his cock as his fingers opened up Erik's ass for the next round. When he could slip three fingers inside, he took Erik's cock as far into his mouth and throat as he could and twisted his fingers to hit that magic spot inside that made Erik see stars.

Erik came with a hoarse shout, shooting down Ben's throat as his hole clenched around his fingers. When he had completely shot his load, Ben licked his cock clean before pushing Erik's knees apart and sliding between them.

"I love you." Ben kissed Erik and let him taste himself on his lips. "Let me in."

Erik raised his hips, and Ben slid inside, snug but not painful.

"Move," Erik whispered.

"Bossy bottom," Ben teased, but he began to fuck Erik slowly, setting up a rhythm. Erik wrapped his legs around Ben's waist, urging him to go faster. It didn't take long for Ben to come after the warmup, and Erik was surprised to find himself half-hard by the time Ben finished.

"That was...perfect," Erik whispered as Ben slipped out and reached for a T-shirt to wipe them up.

Ben leaned in to kiss him. "Told you I could take your mind off things." He tossed the shirt to the floor.

"Mmm...you totally did," Erik agreed.

"Let's get showered and changed, and then we won't be sweaty when we wake up," Ben suggested. Much as Erik hated to get out from beneath the warm sheets, he couldn't fault his partner's argument.

Before long they had cleaned up and gotten ready for bed. Ben threw a hand towel over the wet spot, since neither of them felt like changing the sheets.

"Better?" he asked as Erik slid in beside him. Ben turned toward him and rested his head on Erik's shoulder.

"Much better. This is good, too," Erik told him, long resigned to admitting he enjoyed snuggling.

"Yeah, it's perfect." Ben sounded sleepy and sated. Erik set an alarm for the morning and turned off the light, hoping that his dreams were quiet.

———

"What the hell!" Erik sat bolt upright in bed as the security alarm blared. A glance at the clock said it was a little after three in the morning, still dark.

He threw back the sheets and reached for the Sig he kept in the drawer of his nightstand.

"Don't go out there." Ben reached for his own gun. "Let the cops handle it."

"I will," Erik assured him, "but I want to see what's going on."

A police siren shrieked before they had reached the steps, and Erik wondered if the plainclothes officers kept a vigil through the night. From how quickly the response came after the alarm, he didn't think anyone had time to drive to their location.

Erik kept the gun low as he looked out the window, not wanting to spook the cop. He saw one man on the ground and another cuffing the would-be thief's wrists behind his back. The plainclothes officer flashed his badge, and Erik set the gun aside, motioning for Ben to do the same.

He deactivated the alarm and opened the door. The smell of vomit and feces assaulted Erik's nose, and he realized that the robber lay in his own filth. Erik didn't recognize the intruder.

"I saw him go for the door, and the alarm went off," the cop said, getting to his feet. "All of a sudden, the guy starts puking and shitting, and then he curled up in a ball."

"Well, that kept him from running away." Erik didn't offer an explanation. "Sorry for the mess."

The cop wrinkled his nose. "I'm putting down a tarp in the back before he gets in my car." He hauled the man to his feet. "Someone will get in touch with you in the morning. Try to get some sleep."

Erik and Ben watched the cop wrap the thief in a plastic sheet before maneuvering him into the back of the car and driving away.

"Well, that proves the protection spells worked," Erik said.

Ben slipped on shoes and jumped down to the side of the steps where he could reach a garden hose. After blasting the concrete clean and sluicing away what spread to the sidewalk, Ben turned off the water and came back inside, carefully leaving his shoes on the mat.

"I need another shower," he mumbled.

"Go ahead," Erik told him. "I'll close up here and reset the alarm.

We can get Alessia to fully re-establish the wards tomorrow, but I can do enough tonight that anyone who makes another try will be sorry."

He checked the door for damage, reset the locks and alarm, then trundled up the steps. The warm glow from their earlier lovemaking had dimmed, leaving anxious exhaustion in its place.

"Take a deep breath," Ben coaxed when he slipped in beside Erik. "You're safe. I'm safe. The store wasn't damaged. A cop really was looking out for us. Maybe we'll get some clues about who's after us. At the very least, that's one guy who isn't likely to make a second attempt. Try to let it go and get some sleep."

Erik kissed Ben. "I'll do my best, no guarantees. Stay close."

"Always," Ben promised.

They had barely gotten through their morning bathroom routine the next day before Erik's phone rang.

"Hendricks here," the chief greeted him gruffly. "I'm downstairs. We need to talk."

"I'll be right down," Erik told him. "Don't try to open the door before I turn off the system."

"You gonna tell him?" Ben asked as Erik ran a comb through his still-wet hair.

"I will. Doesn't mean he'll believe me. Depends on whether he thinks magic or spontaneous intestinal distress is harder to accept."

Erik hurried downstairs and disabled the security system. He opened the door and found Hendricks standing on the sidewalk, well off the steps.

"It's safe to come in." Erik stood aside to let him enter.

"Officer Calvin said he saw a man approach the door and move to pick the lock. Just as the officer was going to intervene, the man doubled over and started throwing up, followed by him losing control of his bowels," Hendricks recapped. "He didn't recover until this morning. Want to explain the timing on that?"

"Magic."

Hendricks gave him a skeptical look, although Erik thought the chief had to have anticipated the response. "Come again?"

"In addition to a top-grade security system, the building is heavily warded, protected with sigils and spells to keep out intruders with ill intent," Erik said, as if nothing about his answer was unusual.

"You're saying that was magic?"

"It's a non-lethal way to incapacitate someone who clearly meant us harm." Erik shrugged. "It will wear off in a couple more hours. And while I imagine he'll feel lousy and be dehydrated, there are no lasting effects. Although I suspect he won't be quick to try again—which is the whole idea."

Hendricks regarded him for a moment as if trying to make sure Erik wasn't playing with him.

"Magic," he repeated, clearly wrestling with the idea.

"You don't have to include that in your report," Erik supplied helpfully. "Just chalk it up to severe, spontaneous intestinal distress. Something he ate really didn't agree with him and picked a bad time to create a reaction."

Hendricks gave a non-committal *humpfh.* "You think he was after that damned window?"

"Damned" might be the right word for it, Erik thought.

"We haven't had any new acquisitions since I bought the window, given how bad the weather's been, and nothing else we bought recently has been out of the ordinary—definitely not magical," Erik replied.

Hendricks twitched at the "M-word" but didn't object. "Any idea who might have sent the thief?"

"Guesses, but nothing solid," Erik replied. "Do you know who the thief is?"

Hendricks sighed. "Rudy Cosentino. He's got a rap sheet as long as my arm. Not local talent; usually causes trouble in Wildwood. Bit player, thug-for-hire. Definitely someone who would be considered disposable if they hired him for a job and it went wrong."

"Like last night, if the magic had played for keeps." Erik hadn't considered that the attempt might have been a dry run to see how good their protections were.

"Could be," Hendricks admitted.

"Shit, no pun intended." Erik ran a hand back through his hair. "We can increase the protections and still keep it non-lethal, but it would be better for everyone if I had specialists move the window to a much more secure facility."

"I'd be inclined to agree with you, if that didn't mean losing track of it forever, which is part of the service if I understood you correctly." The chief raised an eyebrow.

"That's usually considered a perk, not a detraction."

"Come up with anyone likely to want the window badly enough to hire an out-of-town tough to try to steal it?" Hendricks asked. "Because someone who would believe that the window was really haunted might also believe you could—and would—protect the store with magic."

"Not yet," Erik replied. "We've made some quiet inquiries with people who might know."

Hendricks looked like he might be getting a headache. His eyes squinted and his forehead creased. "Why is it never simple with you two? We've got a big event coming up in town, and we can't have a Mafia war brewing. Not that there's ever a good time for that," he added under his breath.

"We totally understand," Ben jumped in. "We want this settled and done as quickly and quietly as possible."

Hendricks looked skeptical, but Erik hoped their candor had won some of the chief's trust, even if he didn't like what he heard.

"Let me talk to the lawyers about permitting you to hand off the window to a third party," Hendricks told them. "Do you think your person could put it in safekeeping for a while before burying it forever, in case we get a lead in the case?"

"I can ask." Given the dangerous magic entwined with the window, Erik thought the Alliance was unlikely to want to give it back.

"Much obliged." Hendricks's comment was sarcastic but not mean-spirited, and Erik thought the other man looked tired. Getting ready for a large event and an influx of people was probably already a scheduling nightmare, without worrying about Mafia complications.

"If we get anything useful out of Cosentino, I'll let you know," Hendricks told them as he turned to go. "And if you find a hot lead, I'm counting on reciprocity."

"We will keep you in the loop," Erik promised, making a few mental exceptions.

Hendricks looked skeptical, but he wished them a good day, told them to stay out of trouble, and headed back to the station.

"That was fun. Not," Ben observed.

"At least he isn't dragging us into the station and making us give statements," Erik said. "Maybe he's worried about what we'd say."

FOUR

BEN

After breakfast, Erik called Haley and Monty to arrange times to get together and asked Alessia to reinforce the shop's protections, then he and Ben headed to the oldest cemetery in Cape May.

"Grant Samuels, the collector from Wildwood, was a very wealthy man who made his money in shipping and freight," Erik said as they drove. "Suspected to be a witch."

"Those are businesses that historically have a lot of ties to organized crime," Ben supplied. "But if he lived in Wildwood, why was he buried in Cape May?"

"Good question, and I have no idea," Erik admitted. "If I had to guess, I'd say that since he was a witch, he might have thought that Cold Spring Cemetery held more magical energy than the options in Wildwood because it's much older."

"I guess that's possible," Ben said.

"Wildwood is known for its haunted attractions, fake vampire castles, zombie mazes, and that sort of thing," Erik added. "But Cape May is one of the most truly haunted towns in the Eastern U.S. Maybe that mattered to Samuels as well."

"Because he didn't want to be lonely after he croaked?" Ben

grinned. "I guess I've heard stranger things. But what's the connection to the Tiffany glass?"

"The Tiffany cemetery markers," Erik replied. "Samuels already owned an angel statue that was a real Tiffany. By the time he commissioned his own headstone, the Tiffany company was no longer doing that kind of work, so he hired a talented stone carver to do one for him in the same style."

"Do you expect to find a clue of some sort at the grave?" Ben asked.

"I don't know what we'll find. Maybe nothing. I'd be surprised if Samuels's ghost was still hanging around, but he might if he had a strong enough purpose," Erik replied. "If we can't find him there, maybe Haley can summon his spirit."

Cold Spring Cemetery dated back to the 1700s. Ben felt the hair on his arms rise, which usually meant strong ghosts close by. He saw Erik stiffen as soon as they got out of the car and guessed his partner also sensed the spirits.

"Ghosts?" he confirmed.

Erik nodded. "Lots of them. The cemetery was started by the people who founded the village of Cold Spring. It's a living history museum now, but back in the day, those early settlers braved hurricanes and pirates to put down stakes. The historic village area is said to be very haunted."

"Isn't everything around here?" Ben asked, only partly in jest.

"It certainly feels like it," Erik replied. "I've always been interested in going to the Village when it's open, but so far there have been other priorities."

Ben snickered at the understatement. Since they both moved to Cape May, hauntings and unfinished business from their prior jobs kept them busy.

The old cemetery wasn't fancy, just row upon row of old headstones surrounded by an iron fence, right beside a brick church. They parked and got out, walking toward the entrance.

"You know we're being followed," Ben said quietly.

"Yeah, since we left the shop. Pretty sure it's the plainclothes detective," Erik said. "If it isn't, we're likely to find out soon."

No one else was around, so if their tail wasn't a protector, he was likely to make his move despite them being on consecrated ground.

Erik pulled out his phone and opened the cemetery map he had found earlier. Then he navigated toward the plot where Samuels was buried.

The headstone was almost stark compared to others known to have been actually designed by Tiffany. An Art Deco-styled cross surrounded by the carved lilies that were a hallmark of Tiffany projects marked Samuel's final resting place, with his dates and name on the opposite side of the stone from the carving.

"There's no angel," Ben said when they arrived.

Erik spotted a small placard on a stake and moved to read it. "They moved the angel to the St. Expeditus by the Sea compound," he reported.

"And if it had magic, the nuns would be able to deal with it," Ben said.

"That, too." Erik went still, and Ben stood quietly, waiting to see if Erik would receive a vision. Their plainclothes tail stayed near the cemetery entrance, giving them space but still close enough in case of trouble. Ben didn't see any other living people inside the graveyard.

"Grant Samuels, are you here?" Erik murmured. The wind picked up, sharply cold. Ben didn't know if that was a response or just coincidence.

Several minutes passed and no vision manifested. Erik shoved his hands into his pockets and shrugged. "Nothing. No vision, no visible ghost," he told Ben. "You?"

Ben shook his head.

"Maybe Monty or Haley will have better luck."

"Do you think it's worth arranging a visit to the convent to see the angel statue?" Ben asked.

"Probably," Erik replied as they headed back to the car. He saluted the cop, who nodded in response and got back in his vehicle. "It might not have any clues, but since we aren't entirely sure what we're looking for, I'm hoping we know it when we see it."

They swung by the beach on their way back into town. Rain had held off so far, but ominous dark clouds hung on the horizon, threatening more storms.

"Just couldn't stay away, huh?" Monty joked when he opened the lighthouse door.

"I'll never turn down an excuse to go to the beach," Ben replied.

"Me, neither. But we also wanted to see how the ghost situation was responding to the storms," Erik added.

Monty's gaze slid past them to where Ben suspected Jon's spirit stood. "Jon says the energy has been weird. Not as bad as when there have been hurricanes, but it makes him feel jangly, like too much sugar and coffee."

"Stronger?" Erik pressed.

Monty hesitated as if listening and then nodded. "Yes."

"Picking up anything potentially dangerous from the old railroad tracks or the military locations?" Erik asked.

Cape May had been an important strategic location during World War II. People still told stories about German U-boats prowling the shore or a spy being shot off the top of the tall lookout tower that kept a watch for enemy ships. A solid concrete bunker anchored the shore, which once housed a gun battery and a radio transmitting station, all now decommissioned.

Monty stopped to listen, and Ben figured Jon was giving him an earful.

"The ghosts haunting the railroad tracks aren't like the usual beach spirits from drownings or boating accidents," Monty explained. "They're angry because the 'accidents' that killed them were usually due to companies cutting corners on safety or not protecting them from dangerous materials. Of course, the people responsible have been dead for decades, and the companies are long gone."

"Are they dangerous? Can they find some kind of peace?" Ben asked.

"We keep an eye on them," Monty replied. "Usually, they leave the tourists alone. With all the storm energy, they've been more active, but so far they haven't threatened or hurt anyone."

"As for finding peace, Jon and I have sent all the active ghosts who will go, either to the convent or on to the other side," Monty told them. "Some repeaters remain, but I don't think they are strong enough to cause problems."

It still surprised Ben that Cape May had few wartime ghosts, given all the fortifications. Then again, the bunker and watch tower never saw the level of combat that their builders feared.

"Jon says that at various times, the Mob used both the bunker and the tower for dead drops," Monty reminded them. "Not recently, but also not that long ago."

Monty paused again. "Jon says you should talk to the nuns. They take in wayward and lost spirits and have gathered a lot of them off the beach over the years. Jon never wanted to go with them, but the nuns still come through every so often looking for more wandering souls."

Ben and Erik exchanged a look. "I don't know if they could tell us anything, even if they have ghosts there with information. Seal of the confessional and all that," Erik said.

"Can't hurt to ask," Monty said. "Maybe there's a ghost or two who want to unburden themselves before they go on."

"I hadn't considered that," Erik replied.

"The nuns aren't just mediums, right?" Ben tried to remember what he had read. "They also have pretty strong defensive magic, if I remember right." The sisters didn't mingle much with the residents of Cape May, but they weren't complete recluses when they could be of help.

"Jon says that during the war they cared for the injured and the families of soldiers from the area who were killed or missing in action," Monty relayed. "And later, after he was a ghost himself, Jon says he realized that some of the nuns must have magic or precognition because they served as unofficial advisors to the military when the threat level was high."

"Huh. Spying nuns," Ben said. "That's a new one."

"We were hoping they would see us, because they have a Tiffany angel statue that belonged to Samuels," Erik said. "No idea if it ties in with the window drama, but it's worth checking."

"How is Haley handling your brand of weirdness?" Monty asked with a grin.

"We've kinda thrown her into the deep end with a few things, and she's dealt with it like a pro," Erik replied proudly.

"She's good, and her schedule is more flexible than mine," Monty said. "I also want to introduce you to a priest who has helped us out when we needed an exorcism or help with some really bad mojo. Father Dennis Moore. He knows about the supernatural and believes in it. Has some magic in addition to the power of the Church. I'll text you his contact information and let him know you'll be in touch."

"Thank you," Ben said. "I'm hoping the situation doesn't escalate, but if it does, we'll need all the help we can get." Erik nodded in agreement.

"We'll holler if anything interesting happens around here," Monty promised. "Jon's on the lookout. Keeps him out of trouble."

Monty reacted as Jon's ghost elbowed him. Ben and Erik laughed.

They left with a promise to get together again soon. The cop tailing them had waited near the cars, in a spot where he had a clear view of the beach around the lighthouse. He waited for Ben and Erik to get back in their car before doing the same and following them as they pulled away.

"I guess sending the angel statue to the nuns makes sense in a lot of ways," Ben said as Erik drove toward Haley's shop. "It would be safer from art thieves than in the cemetery, especially since the nuns have magic to protect it. And if the statue had any mojo, the nuns could contain it."

Erik nodded. "Angels were often seen as helpers or messengers. The nuns themselves have also certainly fit that description over the years."

He paused. "I emailed a friend of mine who specializes in forensic accounting and asked for a favor. I'm hoping he can find out who the biggest purchasers from the Commodore Wilson liquidation auction were, and cross-reference that with the ones where Bellamy handled the sale."

"You figure that one of them also got away with the dome, since they would have had a lot of packing crates?" Ben asked.

"Worth a shot. Want to bet the top bidders also were mobbed up the wazoo?"

"That's a sucker's bet," Ben replied. "Of course they were."

Erik was quiet for a moment. "That evangelist who was the last owner owed many people a lot of money, including the Mafia," he mused. "Maybe he promised them the dome toward what he owed, or they just decided to take it to pay down the debt."

"Not legal, but certainly possible," Ben agreed. "And since the dome would be damn near priceless, sneaking it out avoided paying taxes."

"That, too."

Signs about the Awesome Autumn Festival had sprung up everywhere. Ben knew he would feel more enthusiastic if a Mob shootout wasn't still a possibility. Although he would normally be looking forward to the roles he and Erik had agreed to play, the preparations seemed more like a distraction at the moment.

Erik parked down the block from Haley's apartment, where she also held psychic readings. Their plainclothes bodyguard found a spot nearby.

"At least we should get a heads up if anyone is following the guy who follows us," Ben noted with a nod to the cop. "And if he thinks there are sketchy people scoping out the store."

"I didn't want to bring anyone else into this because of the organized crime angle, but if we can make contact with some of the spirits, it could fill in some of the missing information and maybe prevent this from getting to be a bigger deal," Erik said.

"Do you think Haley is a strong enough ghost whisperer to handle this kind of stuff?" Ben asked.

"I guess we'll find out," Erik said.

"Just like getting a witness to spill their guts. Sometimes one cop will make a stronger connection than another, and if the informant feels more comfortable, they say more," he added.

Ben had certainly seen that play out with human witnesses and guessed there was no reason for ghosts to be different. *Ghosts are still people—just dead ones.*

Haley had a quiet table ready when they showed up. "I made fresh tea," she told them as she ushered them inside and closed the door, leading them to the back room. "Always helps to soothe the nerves."

She poured cups for all of them, then sat facing Ben and Erik. Candles flickered on the table.

"Before we go further, I need to ask, do you really want to know?" Haley gave a pointed look to Erik then Ben. "Because you can't un-know once I tell you, and that may make you a target for bad people."

"Yes, Erik said. "We need answers, and bad people are already targeting us. That wouldn't be new."

Haley laughed. "If you knew half of what the ghosts tell me on a regular basis, you'd put me in witness protection. People who didn't get their sins off their chest before they die want someone to hear their secrets afterward."

"How do you deal with that?" Ben asked, intrigued.

"If the new information can help solve a crime, find a missing person, or save someone, I will make an anonymous tip to authorities," Haley replied. "If it's just someone getting bad choices or indiscretions off their chest, I don't. Confessing to murder? Yes. Confessing to an affair? Nope."

She paused to sip her tea. "It's something I had to wrestle with for a long time. But no human harm can come to the ghost; they told me of their own free will, and doing my best to prevent more damage or right a wrong is the closest to absolution I can give them."

"That makes a lot of sense," Erik said. "I've used the information that ghost informants have provided numerous times to solve cases, find stolen goods, and identify criminals. It's not admissible in court, but the ghosts' information usually leads me to something that *can* be used."

"And given what we talked about last time, I'm guessing this has to do with the Mafia and old cold cases?"

"Yup," Ben said with a grin. "I guess we're predictable."

"I heard about the guy who tried to break into your shop, and that makes me suspect that the two recent murders the cops aren't saying much about have something to do with it all," Haley said.

Erik and Ben took turns explaining more of the basics of the case, with the stolen dome, the haunted window, the known Mafia ties, and what they had pieced together from research.

"You boys managed to step in it." Haley shook her head. "And it sounds like the Commodore Wilson is the biggest ghost. But I have to ask, if the dome has been missing for thirty years, why does it matter now? I'd think you would be glad to have it out of Cape May. Good riddance."

"Yeah, we probably should feel that way," Ben replied. "But since there have been two murders connected to Tiffany windows, and one of those victims helped to sell off the dome from the Commodore Wilson, it seems like it's not going to end until we figure out what's going on."

"You think someone wants to use the dome for some sort of magic?" Haley asked.

"We know the panel has dark energy," Erik said. "Domes concentrate power. It might be able to boost the efforts of a spellcaster with bad intentions."

Haley nodded after a moment to think over what he had said. "I guess that's possible. We draw warded circles and create energy domes on a much smaller scale, and for very brief uses."

"The storms are already boosting energy," Ben added. "And someone is interested enough in the Tiffany dome that they've killed twice. That's definitely not the kind of person we want 'boosted.'"

"Okay. You've made your case," Haley agreed.

"We want to contact Grant Samuels," Erik said. "There's a chance he knows more than we do about the dome."

"No guarantee Samuels will show, but let's give it a try," Haley said.

They joined hands, and Haley slipped into a trance. "Grant Samuels. We call to you. Please speak with us."

Silence stretched for a minute, then two. Just as Ben thought Samuels had refused to talk with them, he felt a cold breeze that raised his hackles.

"It's Samuels," Haley said. "He's here, and I don't think he's happy about it. I'll let you know what he says."

"A man is dead because he bought a haunted stained-glass window from your estate. Who would kill for that and why?" Haley asked, but from the delay, Ben guessed that Samuels didn't answer right away.

"The Collector, or The Oligarch. He doesn't know their real names. Powerful crime bosses who coveted art, especially stained glass," Haley repeated.

"Do you know what happened to the Tiffany dome from the Commodore Wilson hotel?"

Another pause, longer this time. "He wanted to bid, and they said they would kill him if he did," Haley relayed.

"They?"

"The Collector and The Oligarch. He didn't want to know who won. It touched off a Mob war," Haley murmured.

"The angel statue, does it have magic?" Erik blurted.

Ben felt the cold weight of the ghost's presence.

"It can amplify resonance," Haley told Ben what the ghost said.

"Who haunts the window?" Haley asked and waited for an answer.

"Arkadi Mikhailov, the witch who originally commissioned it. The one who wrote the grimoire." Haley looked distressed at the revelation as she repeated the information. She glanced at Erik and Ben, checking to see if they had other questions. Erik sensed that the ghost had probably answered out of boredom and was running out of patience. Both men shook their heads.

"Thank you for speaking with us. Go in peace," Haley told the spirit.

Erik felt a shift in the energy, and knew the ghost was gone.

"I think that was a one-shot deal," Haley told Ben and Erik. "He doesn't want to hear from us again."

They didn't speak until Haley had sage-smudged the area and done a purification ritual. The ghost carried a darkness with it that made Ben want to bathe in holy water.

"What did you make of that?" Haley asked. Ben sensed she had some strong opinions but was waiting to hear theirs first.

"Creepy." Ben spoke up first. "If I had walked into an empty house and got the sensations he was putting off, I'd have salted his ass or high-tailed it out of there."

Erik nodded. "He wasn't a good man, and he didn't care. But we got what we came for, a couple of names we didn't have before, and an answer about the window that got Peter Randolph killed."

"Those two names, The Collector and The Oligarch, sounded like something out of an action movie," Haley noted.

"Welcome to our lives," Ben said with a sigh.

"Hey, it keeps things interesting," Haley replied. "People who want to say nice things to ghosts and parted on good terms just think of them or leave flowers at their graves. They only come to me when it's a difficult conversation." She paused. "Although I've got to admit, the folks you look for are a bit more interesting than most."

"Thank you," Erik said. "I know ghosts with dark energy are more of a drain than usual. But it's for a good cause, I swear."

"If you can head off a Mob war before the fall festivals, I'm all in favor," Haley said. "I just moved here, and I'd like to keep the place intact. And I don't scare off easily. Just call me whenever you need me."

They thanked her profusely and paid extra for the session before heading out to the car.

"Do you think the stained glass has its own magic?" Ben asked as they drove home, nudging Erik out of his thoughts.

"If you had asked me before this, I would have said no," Erik replied. "Now…I'm not sure. There are paintings and statues reputed to have magic, whether people call it that or credit divine intervention. Why not windows? Guess I need to do some research."

"That name he gave us, the man in the haunted panel. It was Russian. Does that mean Bratva's going to be involved?" Ben didn't hide his worry.

"Maybe they were always going to turn up, and that just gave us an early warning," Erik said. "Especially with someone who goes by 'The Oligarch' involved, I'm guessing there's a long history."

"And from what Samuels's ghost said, 'The Collector' is from a rival crime family as well as rich and unethical," Ben mused.

"Which shouldn't be a surprise given the Commodore Wilson's past. Over the years, there were Mafia-sponsored gatherings at the hotel using thinly-veiled aliases." Erik drummed his fingers on the steering wheel. "I just feel like we've missed something, and I don't want it to bite us on the ass."

Ben glanced in the side mirror. "Still got the cop on our tail. I wonder what he makes of all this. We aren't typical of what he's probably used to shadowing."

"We haven't hit one bookie, gambling joint, or house of ill repute all week," Erik replied.

"I used to be a private investigator, remember? That job definitely shows you the seamier side of life. I thought I was pretty jaded from being a cop, but being a detective takes that to a whole new level."

"When I wasn't dealing with greedy billionaires and dishonest art dealers, I was appraising art that had been bought with literal blood money," Erik replied. "I might have seen a richer level of scum than you did, but I had a good reason for wanting to get out."

"I'm sorry," Ben said. "So far, we haven't gotten very far out."

Erik shrugged. "We have unique skills, and if we want to keep our adopted town safe, we need to use those abilities. Great power, great responsibility, yada yada."

"Yeah, I feel the same way. But it's a lot more excitement than I bargained for," Ben said.

Erik reached over and took his hand. "At least we're in it together. That makes all the difference."

Ben squeezed his hand. "Absolutely."

Both had come to Cape May after disastrous breakups that had left them wondering if they would ever find the right partner. As far as Ben was concerned, Erik was worth all the danger.

Ben spotted the woman sitting on the steps when Erik parked the SUV. "Looks like we've got company."

Trinkets' magical protections responded to lock picking, attempts to break in by force or magic, and physical harm to the store. That meant that packages and mail could still be delivered safely, and someone coming by with innocent intent after store hours could ring the doorbell or knock gently without getting whammied.

"Can I help you?" Erik asked as they approached the petite woman in a nun's gray habit who rose as they approached.

"Erik Mitchell and Ben Nolan?" she asked. When they nodded, she extended her hand in greeting. "Nice to meet you. I'm Sister Mary Barbara from the St. Expeditus Society. We need to talk."

Erik unlocked the door and released the physical and magical alarm systems. They welcomed Sister Mary Barbara into the shop, and Ben motioned toward the seats around a small table where Erik appraised new items.

"Please, have a seat," Ben said. "Can we make you a cup of tea?"

"Thank you, but no. Maybe a glass of water," Sister Mary Barbara replied.

Ben went to get the water as Erik and the sister took their seats. He joined them minutes later, and the nun sipped the water with a nod of thanks.

"Monty and Jon said we needed to talk to folks at the convent," Erik said. "But you've beaten us to it."

She laughed, and her eyes sparkled. "Hard to surprise folks who are seers and mystics. How much do you know about St. Expeditus by the Sea?"

Erik leaned back in his chair. "Probably not nearly as much as we should," he admitted. "The building started out as a hotel and was reused a couple of times, including by the military during World War II, before becoming a convent."

"A very unusual type of convent," Ben joined in. "Taking in stray ghosts that aren't ready to move on."

Sister Mary Barbara smiled. "You've got the basics. Over the years, we have come out of seclusion when the community needed us to help with emergencies, and during wartime we used our paranormal abilities to help the cause. But we prefer to keep to our studies and intervene in a less public, more supernatural way."

"Do I take that to mean that you serve as guardians, after a fashion?" Erik asked.

She nodded. "In our own way. We can't prevent all dangers, or keep away everything evil, but where we can give a *nudge* in the right direction, we try to make a difference."

Ben found that idea vaguely reassuring.

"How did the convent coexist with the Commodore Wilson Hotel?" Erik asked. "You overlapped for most of a century."

"The land beneath the Commodore Wilson is cursed." Sister Mary Barbara confirmed something they already suspected. "When the Order of St. Expeditus purchased the building that became the convent, it did so with the purpose of being a counterbalance."

She paused for a sip of water. "That was our larger mission—to be a guardian against the forces of darkness. We couldn't heal the genius loci beneath the Commodore Wilson or stop everything bad from happening, but we have done our best to avert the worst possibilities and buffer that harmful energy for the sake of the community."

"Wow." Erik looked sincerely impressed. "That's a pretty impressive mission."

She smiled at him. "Not so different from what the two of you have done since moving here, and how Trinkets has served Cape May since it opened."

Ben was surprised at her comment, while Erik appeared thoughtful.

"Trinkets has always gotten dangerous magical items out of circulation, no matter who owned the shop," she added. "St. Expeditus is a sanctuary for troubled ghosts. Much like halfway houses for living people, we provide a place for them to heal and try to prevent them from becoming vengeful or troublesome."

"There's plenty of work like that to go around," Erik replied. "Cape May has ghosts galore."

"Ghosts and mobsters," Sister Mary Barbara said. "Perhaps not as much as Wildwood or Atlantic City, but enough over the decades to weave them into the history of the town. We can't put a psychic fence around Cape May to keep them out, but we do what we can to mitigate."

Given the run-ins with the Mafia he and Erik had since moving to Cape May, Ben didn't want to think what it would have been like without the nuns' mitigation.

"Thank you," Erik replied.

She shrugged off the comment. "It's our mission. Our purpose. We are grateful to make a difference."

"Were you aware of the energy in the Commodore Wilson's Tiffany dome while the building still stood?" Ben asked. "Everything we're dealing with seems to keep coming back to Tiffany windows."

Sister Mary Barbara nodded. "We knew. It was a focal point for ill intent. While the hotel was standing, we did our best to drain the dome's power. When the building was destroyed and the dome removed, it weakened the loci by taking away its nexus."

"You don't think the dome was demolished when they imploded the Commodore Wilson?" Erik asked.

"No. It was far too significant—both as art and as a magical artifact—for that to happen," she said. "There was a powerful storm at that time, much like what we've had lately. Many people wanted to purchase the dome, but it came down to two obsessed men with Mafia money and connections. We were barely able to avert a war, and even so, violence occurred."

"Do you know who ended up with the dome?" Ben questioned. "Because no one has seen it for more than thirty years."

"No, and I don't know where it is, although I'm certain it still exists. Someone with strong magic has wrapped it in spells to keep it hidden," Sister Mary Barbara answered.

"What do you know about a dark witch named Arkadi Mikhailov?" Erik asked. "We got a tip from a ghost that he might have played a role in what's unfolding."

Her expression darkened. "He was not a good man. A very powerful witch, but he used his abilities to cause great harm. Why do you ask?"

Erik explained about the Tiffany stained-glass panel and the two murders related to it and possibly to the dome, as well as what they had gleaned from Samuels's ghost earlier in the day at Haley's séance.

"Grant Samuels was one of the people whose impact we tried to limit over the years," she said. "We did our best to keep him out of Cape May's affairs."

"We know people who contain dangerous magical objects that can't be destroyed," Erik said. "As soon as the police chief lets us, we'll be having them take the window and make sure it can't hurt anyone again. We'll send the dome on as well if we can find it."

"We are aware of the Alliance and the Briggs Society," Sister Mary Barbara said. "We also know Sorren, the honorable vampire who works with them. Our paths have crossed many times over the years."

"Was the Tiffany dome magical in itself, aside from the energy it focused or absorbed from the genius loci?" Erik asked.

"I believe so. You of all people should know that artwork can be infernal as well as sacred." She confirmed Ben's suspicion that she knew their backgrounds.

"There is a very large dome in Chicago that has arcane protective symbols along with those of the zodiac. Other windows use iconography to anchor magic, or patterns in the way the glass is pieced together to work spells into the window's structure itself," the nun added.

Ben's eyebrows rose. He had never considered that possibility, and now he viewed the window in their safe with even more skepticism.

"Really?" Erik asked, eyes alight, and Ben knew that his art historian partner was intrigued.

Sister Mary Barbara nodded. "Depending on the glassmaker, it could involve alchemy, numerology, or astronomy. Most of the windows are mundane, but the ones that were designed to channel energy and power are a lot more than just a pretty picture."

"Can you tell us more?" Erik pressed, and Ben guessed he was thinking about the window in the safe.

"I'm not an expert, but I can tell you what I know," she replied. "For example, the colors in the glass come from substances that also have arcane resonance. Cobalt is said to influence emotional healing and creativity, while cadmium can create a beacon to attract the energy that is desired.

"Antimony is linked to protection, purification, and clairvoyance," she continued. "Chromite influences strength, while sulfur is used for banishing. And the lead that holds it all together creates a neutral space to keep things in or out."

"I never thought about the construction of a window being magical," Erik replied. "Just the image."

"When the glassmaker is also a powerful witch, all the pieces reinforce each other," Sister Mary Barbara said. "The image. The direction that the window faces, especially if it catches the sun or moon at key ritual times. The number of pieces, repeating patterns, and protective sigils, especially when they're worked into the borders where no one notices. It all works together under a master's hand."

"Was Louis Comfort Tiffany a witch?" Ben asked.

The nun shrugged. "That's debated. If he wasn't, then he enabled powerful witches to create windows that went out under his name."

"He also did stonework." Erik looked like this new information about stained glass windows had thrown him for a loop. "Headstones, mausoleums, and carved figures like the angel statue. How did those factor into the magic?"

"Modern people think statues and carvings are just decorative," she replied. "Ancient people knew they could be more. Sacred statues were sometimes thought to be manifestations of the deities they represented, a temporary 'shell' for their energy.

"Over the centuries, people believed that carvings amplified power or provided protective warding. Stone carvers who could create images that were both beautiful and imbued with magic were revered," Sister Mary Barbara explained.

"Was it really Tiffany himself doing the carving, or someone under his name?" Ben asked.

"Both, perhaps," the nun said. "The man was, by all accounts, extremely gifted in many regards, but I don't think one person could personally create everything that came out of his studio during his lifetime. But he might have contributed key magical elements that a trusted artist completed."

"That would turn the art world upside-down if it became widely known and people actually believed it," Erik mused. "But it makes sense, especially about commissioned pieces."

Ben thought back to the windows in the Catholic church where he grew up, and the ones he had seen since then. He knew he would never look at them the same way again.

"Houses of worship are places where all those elements come together and amplify each other," Sister Mary Barbara said. "Ritual and incantation. Sacred space. Windows, carvings, vestments, blessed food and drink. There's a reason even skeptics can be aware of energy in a place like that. But coupled with belief and intention, and the ability to work magic, you've got the potential for a nexus of power. Then realize that many holy places were intentionally built in locations believed to have special energy, and you start to see why it's not just your imagination that there's something otherworldly in that space."

"Mausoleums and cemeteries are, at least metaphorically, portals to the afterlife," Erik mused. "A different kind of energy, especially with necromancy."

"Wardings to keep bad things out, and carvings to help the deceased find their way. Blessings and protections or, in some cases, bindings. There are many old ways woven into our modern traditions, even if we don't recognize them." Sister Mary Barbara picked up her water glass as she watched them.

Ben's head spun as he thought about all the funerals and graveside ceremonies he had attended, and the times he and Erik had been obliged to dig up a body to stop a greater threat. He made a mental note to talk to Erik and Alessia afterward about how to factor this new information into their plans.

"Why was the angel statue moved from the cemetery to the convent?" Erik asked. "I know the public story is about protecting it from the elements or vandals. But after everything you've told us, I'm betting there's more to it than that."

"To protect the statue, and also protect the world *from* the statue," Sister Mary Barbara replied. "It channeled enough power to be a tempting prize. Cape May has earned its reputation for being haunted. But it would be worse without the precautions put in place and maintained by the town's supernatural community. That includes intentionally landscaping our cemeteries to reduce negative spirit energy."

Ben's skepticism must have shown in his expression. "It's not perfect," the nun reproved him, "but it would be much worse without the measures."

Ben's Catholic school training came back, unbidden, and he ducked his head. "Sorry."

Erik snickered, and Sister Mary Barbara smiled as if she could guess the history behind his expression. "This isn't information that we share with everyone. There's a reason you didn't know."

"Over the years, we've beautified our local cemeteries in ways that help confused spirits move on and neutralizes those with ill intent. Next time you go, notice the juniper, sage, mugwort, lavender, and rosemary plantings," she said. "Those are all plants that cleanse and protect, intentionally planted."

"I'm guessing that the bequeathed statuary and other elements also play a role?" Erik asked, and Ben wasn't going to be surprised if his partner hauled him out to see for himself as soon as their guest was gone.

"Not all, but definitely some of them," Sister Mary Barbara confirmed. "No one without training thinks twice about the sense of calm most people feel in a cemetery. Some of it comes from those decorations."

"I'd hate to think about what a spookapalooza this town would be without all those interventions," Ben replied.

"You wouldn't like it," she assured him.

With that, Sister Mary Barbara set her empty glass aside and stood. "I thank you for the hospitality. It's good to make your acquaintance. We are very aware of how much both of you have risked to protect this town. We've quietly helped when we could, even if you couldn't tell. With the coming storm, we will make every effort to avert harm. Call me if you need me."

She handed a card with the convent's contact information to Erik, then made her exit with a nod and a smile.

Ben watched her walk down the sidewalk and head toward the beachfront convent.

"That blew my mind a little," he admitted.

Normally, that phrasing would have invited a suggestive comment, but Erik looked equally shaken.

"Yeah, I'm going to need to think about all that for a while," Erik agreed.

"I don't like the weather forecast." Susan cradled a hot cup of coffee in her hands. "Do you have plywood to board up the front windows if it really gets bad?"

Susan had insisted on stopping in to check on Ben and Erik, and had brought along a chicken noodle casserole and a pan of sweet rolls for dinner "to keep their spirits up."

Erik looked up from his computer. "Do you really think it might?"

The rain made for a slow morning. A few people called to schedule appraisals on recent estate purchases, but no one stopped in, and Erik didn't see any foot traffic on the sidewalk. Then again, walking in this storm would be more like swimming.

"It wouldn't be the first time," Susan remarked. "The last big hurricane hit here in the early 1800s, and people still talk about how the town was cut off by a ten-foot storm surge. A Category 2 hit in 1903, and then in 1944, a series of bad storms wiped the whole community of South Cape May right into the ocean. It never rebuilt."

Erik's eyebrows rose. "Wow."

"Old timers still talk about the Nor'easter of 1962. Took out the boardwalk, convention hall, and a bunch of shops," Susan went on.

"Although Hurricane Sandy mostly missed us, even though we were told to evacuate."

"I guess we've been lucky since I moved here," Erik admitted. "Do you think there's plywood in the storage area?"

"Pretty likely," Susan said. "Go have a look, and I'll stay here in case some sodden soul wanders in from the storm."

He thought they were pretty safe from surprise visitors, but then again, Peter Randolph had shown up with his haunted window in a storm.

Erik didn't often go into that part of Trinkets, unlike the finished storage rooms where they kept stock. The old converted house had an area consistent with trends when it was built, an unfinished space with bare concrete walls that held the furnace and other plumbing and heating essentials. He had been warned by the previous owner not to store anything in the area that would be damaged by humidity or water, so the winter tires for his SUV were the only things he had put there.

Against the far wall, Erik spotted several stained sheets of plywood. They had clearly seen storm water but seemed to be in good enough shape to be nailed in place if necessary.

In all his years of traveling for museums and law enforcement, Erik never worried about storms beyond their impact on his flight schedule. Thinking like the owner of a home and business was new, and he sometimes felt overwhelmed by what he didn't automatically know. That made Susan's insights all the more valuable, since she was a lifelong Cape May resident.

"Yep, we've got plywood," Erik announced when he returned. "Hoping we don't have to use it, but it's good to know. If things weren't so high tech now, I'd suspect the radio station's antennae were getting blown around, considering how the signal keeps going in and out." Given the weather, Erik had tuned to the local station for updates.

"Happens every time there's a storm," Susan agreed with a sigh. "Satellite or antennae, doesn't matter."

Static drowned out the weather report, followed by a high-pitched squeal.

"Buccaneer Radio, mayday. I repeat, mayday." The voice was lost in static again, and then the weather report resumed mid-sentence.

"What was that?" Erik realized Susan had gone pale. "You look like you saw a ghost."

"Heard one." She sounded shaky. "Welcome to another Cape May ghost story and storm tradition."

"What is Buccaneer Radio?" Erik couldn't help being intrigued.

Susan sat and paused before responding. "The seventies were wild around here, just like they were everywhere. There was a guy who had a lot of opinions on everything that was going on: politics, culture, music, and more. He was quite a showman and could pack speaking engagements. But he couldn't be on the radio back then because there were stricter rules than there are now about what you could and couldn't say.

"He bought a decommissioned Navy minesweeper and converted it to an offshore radio station." She chuckled and shook her head. "Quite the publicity stunt, but folks think he really believed he could make a go of it by bringing in donations and advertisers."

"What happened?" Erik tried to imagine how the usually staid Cape May society would have reacted.

"A bad storm came in. His equipment failed, the government served notice that they were going to impound the ship, but before they got there, it capsized and sank," Susan replied. "The way I've heard it, by the time the authorities got there, they saw a life preserver but never found his body. Quite the scandal in its day."

"Give the man credit for originality." Erik laughed.

Susan sobered. "The thing is, hearing the phantom broadcasts is considered an omen around here. Only ever happens when there's a big storm in the offing. I know folks who consider it a signal to pack up and leave town."

Erik frowned. "Ben and I are still new here. Should we go inland? I notice you're still here."

Susan laughed and stood. "Oh, Cole and I would probably be the last to leave and turn the lights out on the way."

"Don't get me wrong, there's a time to give up and get the hell out of Dodge," Susan continued. "There's nothing to be gained by being foolish and staying when it's dangerous. But I don't think we're to that point yet."

Erik looked back to his laptop, where he had been tracking down leads, however thin, that might have a connection to the missing Tiffany dome. "What do you know about the Great Fire of 1878?" he asked, since it seemed clear they weren't likely to get customers.

"The fire was suspicious," Susan said. "No one could prove arson, and the man they arrested wasn't charged, but apparently everyone thought then, and still does, that someone set the fire. It leveled five big hotels and burned forty acres of downtown. On the plus side, disasters like the fire and the big storms made Cape May confront decisions about keeping its Victorian architecture earlier than in many cities." She frowned. "Why? Is it connected to something?"

Erik shrugged. "I'm not sure. There's so much haunted history here, it's difficult to figure out cause and effect."

Susan looked around as if wanting to find something to work on. "Any leads on the stained-glass dome?"

He shook his head. "Nothing yet. Or I should say, lots of leads, but none that panned out yet."

"It may be unlucky, but it certainly was beautiful," Susan said wistfully. "I hope it wasn't destroyed. Surely someone could un-hex it or do an exorcism or something."

Erik chuckled. "I have friends who could certainly give it their best effort. But sort of like the Commodore Wilson and the land under it, sometimes things are bad to the bone."

Susan nodded. "Since we're not likely to get anyone stopping in, I'm going to finish cataloging that last crate from the latest estate sale before Cole comes by to drive me home. At least I'll have it finished before sitting out the storm at home."

"You're supposed to be taking time off until things resolve," Erik reminded her.

"Oh, pish. It's quiet, and if anyone comes in, I can duck out the back. I'm bored." As if it were the only explanation he needed, she walked away.

Erik shook his head and returned his attention to his computer. He knew when to pick his battles.

Erik's phone rang. He didn't recognize the number and was immediately suspicious because the call came from an international source.

"Erik Mitchell," a man's voice said, with a heavy Russian accent. "You do not need to concern yourself with the matter of the Tiffany dome. Turn your attention elsewhere. Buildings can burn, even in the rain, and partners can vanish into the night. None of those things need to come to pass if you mind your own business."

The call ended abruptly. Erik realized his hand shook. He stared at the screen, then turned to his history and snapped a photo to save the number, although he felt certain it came from a burner phone.

Erik felt his heart pound and had a few seconds of light-headedness as the threat sank in. Then he pressed Ben's number. "Ben."

Something in his tone alerted his partner to trouble. "Erik? Are you okay?"

"Please be very careful. Carry your gun. Don't be alone. You're in danger."

"What happened?" Ben immediately slipped into what Erik thought of as "cop mode."

"I just got an international call from someone with a Russian accent warning me off the Tiffany dome and suggesting that they would hurt you and the store if I didn't."

"Shit. Have you told the police?"

"Not yet. I wanted to call you first. Please. Don't take any chances. No piece of art is worth getting killed," Erik begged.

"I can't come home right away because I'm doing a repair check on some of the rental houses with the maintenance team, but I'll leave as soon as I can," Ben promised. "And since someone has your number and knows where you are, that means you're in danger too. Please don't try to be a hero."

"Just come home safely," Erik told him. "It's Bratva. They play for keeps."

"Not my first rodeo, but I'll be careful," Ben said. "You, too."

"Love you," Erik murmured.

"Love you too."

Susan was still out of earshot. Erik wanted to keep her away from danger, and knowing too much was definitely a hazard. He took a couple of deep breaths to calm his nerves and then called Sheriff Hendricks. It wasn't lost on him that the top cop was in his contact list.

"What's up, Mitchell? I assume this isn't social," Hendricks answered in a gruff tone.

"Just got a threatening call from the Russian Mob, figured you'd want to know about it."

Hendricks was silent for a moment. "Not this shit again."

"It's about the Tiffany window."

"The one in your safe?" Hendricks sounded skeptical.

"No, the dome from the Commodore Wilson Hotel that's been missing for thirty years," Erik replied. "I don't have it, and I don't know where it is, but someone thinks I do."

"Want to come down to the station and fill me in?"

"I'd rather do it here, inside the wards," Erik said. "I have a pretty good idea who is behind the call. That way, you can take Susan home and make sure she's safe. I tried to get her to take some time off, but you know your mom."

"I'll be over," Hendricks replied. "And I'll give the plainclothes officer out front a heads up to be even more alert. This used to be a quiet little town." He hung up, and it took Erik a moment to react, lost in his thoughts.

"Is everything okay?" Susan's voice shook him out of his trance.

He turned toward her. "Chief Hendricks is coming here to take my statement about getting a threatening phone call. I want you to leave with him. You were going to stay home for a while to be safe from the storm, but that also goes for avoiding bad people."

She looked at him with a shrewd expression. "Mafia stuff?"

"It's better if you don't know."

"I've lived in New Jersey my whole life. It's hardly a new idea." She gave Erik what he thought of as a "mom" look, assessing his state of mind. "Sit down. I'll get you a fresh cup of coffee. Gather your thoughts before Cole gets here."

Susan brought him coffee and sat quietly with him until a knock came at the door. "I'll let him in." Susan patted his arm. He heard the door open and a muffled conversation, and then the chief came to the break room, looking sodden.

"I hung his slicker up by the door so it could drip," Susan told Erik. "I'll keep sorting that new box of estate stuff."

Erik motioned to the coffee pot. "Go ahead and pour a cup. Thanks for coming over."

"I try to keep international crime syndicates from blowing up my town," Hendricks replied, but he took Erik's suggestion and returned with coffee.

"Now, what's this all about?"

Erik recounted the phone call and shared the number, although he felt certain it would already be disconnected. "Then he threatened the store and Ben. Thick Russian accent. It's got to be someone who works for The Oligarch."

"You mean Vladimir Putin?" Hendricks looked confused.

Despite everything, Erik stifled a chuckle. "No. Russia and the Baltic states have a long history with rich, powerful men who control parts of the economy—legitimately and not-so—and are largely above the law."

"I'm listening."

"His real name is Konstantin Gusev," Erik said. "We crossed paths several times, through proxies, when I worked with Interpol. He grew up wealthy, but his family lost most of their money under Soviet rule. He never lost his expensive tastes."

"You think Gusev called you?" Hendricks clarified.

"No. Gusev always stayed in the shadows. He funded his art habit with his other businesses, drugs, human trafficking, weapons smuggling, and selling information."

"And I imagine he also has ties to Bratva?"

Erik nodded. "All through third parties, so it's an open secret no one can prove. There were rumors linking him to several museum thefts around the world, and that he killed art couriers, rival collectors, and committed arson to cover the robberies."

"One of those rumors was that Gusev had the famous Amber Room that the Nazis stole from the Russians and that disappeared after World War II," Erik continued. "He liked things that were unique and high profile, so the Tiffany dome would fit right in."

"And he decided to call you, why?" Hendricks always seemed surprised to discover more about Erik's background, as if he had difficulty squaring the secret agent level cases he used to pursue with Erik's quiet reinvention as a local antique dealer.

"I stopped one of his attempted thefts and recovered other stolen artwork from his holdings when I was with Interpol," Erik answered. "I testified against him in court, and my team tracked the sources for the laundered money he used to pay for his art on the shadow market. So yeah, he remembers me."

"Well, I've got to give you credit for brass balls." Hendricks sipped his coffee and was quiet for a moment.

Erik had left out that Gusev was a witch, undeterred from using deeply questionable magical traditions to aid his undertakings.

"Do you think he was behind the two murders linked to that 'haunted' window?" Hendricks didn't use finger quotes, but the distinction was clear in his voice.

"No. Too small potatoes for him. Ben and I believe it was the Newark Mob. Specifically, a boss who goes by The Collector."

"What's up with the fancy nicknames? Oligarch. Collector. Pretty fancy for career criminals," Hendricks groused.

"The mobsters who make it to the top have a grandiose streak," Erik told him. "They never get that completely right in the movies."

Erik heard Ben's key in the lock and looked up as his partner came inside and shrugged out of his soaked raincoat.

"I'm guessing you or Nolan know something about this Collector, too?" Hendricks looked like he felt a headache coming on.

Hearing The Collector and The Oligarch's names come up rattled Erik more than he hoped he had let on. It frustrated Erik that despite their best efforts to leave the past behind them, neither he nor his partner could seem to evade the shadows from their former jobs.

"Way too much," Ben answered, having heard the chief's last comment. "What do you want me to tell you?"

Ben came into the break room and poured himself a cup of coffee. He greeted Erik with a peck on the lips and then sat next to him across from Hendricks.

"Erik filled me in about this Oligarch guy. What do I need to know about The Collector? And who the hell comes up with the pretentious nicknames?" Hendricks asked.

"It's part of the mobster ego and posturing," Erik replied. "They've all watched *The Godfather* and *Scarface* too many times."

"The Collector's real name is Remo Barone," Ben said. "His people have been in the Family for generations, and they think they're Mafia gentry. Lots of money, patrons of the arts, they send their kids to expensive colleges and donate a lot of laundered money to things like the ballet and symphony. Which doesn't change the fact that they're stone-cold killers."

"I guess people can ignore a lot when someone writes a big check," Hendricks grumbled.

"Barone must have gone to a lot of art museums growing up, because that's what he stole," Ben continued.

"Erik probably ran across him on international busts. I chased his ass around New Jersey. Sometimes it wasn't about breaking into a museum. The owner of a piece of art died suddenly, and Barone could swoop in and buy the art below market rate. We'd hear later that other potential bidders had their lives threatened if they outbid him," Ben said.

"We saw the same kind of things with his European activity," Erik chimed in. "He managed to dodge the harsher penalties and seemed to consider lesser charges a cost of doing business."

"Barone knew how to set things up so they were legal enough to skate past scrutiny," Ben added.

"And when the money trail or the provenance was shaky, my team and I got pulled in," Erik said.

"Barone isn't going to remember either of us fondly." Ben finished his coffee and set the cup aside.

Erik didn't mention that, like The Oligarch, Barone employed a witch to help cover his tracks and eliminate rivals. He always wondered if that was why Barone's taste in artwork gravitated toward dark supernatural themes.

He had never figured out whether Barone truly liked the art he pursued so ruthlessly, wanted to show off his wealth, or thought that acquiring rare and valuable pieces created legitimacy.

"You both have had very...colorful...lives," Hendricks said. "And I appreciate the briefing. But if no one knows where the Commodore Wilson Tiffany dome is, why the sudden Mafia interest in something that vanished thirty years ago?"

Erik strongly suspected that magic had something to do with it, but he knew that wasn't what Hendricks wanted to hear.

"We've put out some feelers to our contacts who are still in the business," Erik said. "He may have found out that we were looking for it. And the thirtieth anniversary of the Commodore Wilson's implosion may have brought the dome back to people's minds. The haunted window wasn't related, but maybe it was a reminder."

"What are they going to do? Ransack Cape May until they find the dome?" Hendricks asked.

"Only if they can't make Ben or me tell them what they think we know," Erik said. "And they'll take Samuels's window as a consolation prize if they can't get the dome."

Hendricks pushed his now-cold coffee to the side. "Much as I hate to admit it, that means that the two of you are going to have to figure out a plan to send the goons packing with as little bloodshed as possible, preferably before the big festival."

"Thank you for including us in the planning," Ben said, and Erik knew his partner would understand just how big an admission it was on the chief's part.

"I want to be in the loop all the way along," Hendricks added in a stern tone. "Full partner. Don't make me regret this."

"After the threat I got about Ben, I told Susan I thought it would be best if she didn't come in to the store until we got to the bottom of this," Erik said. "And that she take extra care not to become a target. These guys are ruthless, and they would know that threatening her would be leverage."

"I've already invited her to stay with us for a while, spend time with the grandkids," Hendricks replied. "Thank you for thinking about her safety."

"Of course," Erik said. "That's what friends are for."

Susan left with Hendricks after giving Ben and Erik hugs. "Stay safe," she admonished. "I don't want to be away from the store for long."

Once they were gone, Erik locked up and tidied the break room before he and Ben headed up to the apartment.

"Did I miss anything besides a threat on my life?" Ben asked, but his humor fell flat.

Erik gathered him into his arms. "Never joke about that," he growled, and kissed Ben. "I'm going to keep you safe no matter what it takes."

"*We* are going to keep *each other* safe," Ben corrected when they stepped back. "And a good offense is a great defense. We need to start offending."

Erik chuckled at Ben's wording. "That seems to come naturally."

"You know what I meant."

"I got that list of buyers from the Commodore Wilson sale," Erik told Ben as he retrieved the chicken casserole Susan brought and turned on the oven. "I thought we could split it up after dinner and see if any names pop out to us. I don't think we'll find Gusev or Barone themselves, but we might spot an underling. Or someone with minor organized crime connections who could have been working on their own for a third party."

"You think that will help us find the dome?" Ben poured drinks and set the table.

"I've got a hunch that the dome never left this area," Erik replied. "Maybe Cape May proper, but not the general vicinity. Call it intuition."

"Backed up by psychic abilities, that's way more than most people's hunches," Ben said. "Do you have a theory?"

Erik shook his head. "As to why someone would buy the dome and not pass it off to a wealthy purchaser? I'm still working on that."

———

The next morning, Erik woke after a restless sleep. His mind kept turning the questions of the case over and over, and he didn't have a breakthrough to show for it.

"I'll make a fresh pot of coffee," Ben said. "It's going to be a long day. What are you going to work on, since the shop is closed?"

"Maybe it's a wild goose chase, but all that tossing and turning did yield an idea," Erik replied. "I keep thinking, if the dome never left the area, where would it be, and why was it forgotten?"

"I'll bite." Ben made himself a piece of toast with peanut butter. "Why?"

"I haven't gotten that far yet," Erik admitted sheepishly, "But what if someone temporarily stored the boxes at another property they owned, and then for some reason wasn't able to go back and get them?"

"Why would it still be there after all these years?" Ben's background as a cop made him good at punching holes in stories.

"Maybe the property fell on hard times, and no one has been paying a lot of attention," Erik theorized. "That's what I'm going to research today, hotels and other large locations that existed when the Commodore Wilson was demolished that are still standing, but maybe not in good shape or abandoned."

"Promise me you won't go spooking around old cellars alone." Ben gave him a look that silently added *or else*.

Erik waved him away. "No. I'm hoping that I can come up with a couple of options, and then we figure out where to go from there."

"I'm hoping to make a short day of it." Ben set his coffee cup in the sink and took his mostly dry raincoat down from a peg and put it on. "With luck, Jenny and I won't find any leaks or overflowing gutters, and the punch list will be short."

"Stay dry, and keep your eyes open for trouble," Erik warned as he stood to give Ben a kiss.

"I will." Ben tapped the holster at his belt. "And I've got my Glock."

Erik sincerely hoped Ben didn't need the weapon, but he felt relieved that his partner had taken the warning seriously enough to go armed, just in case.

"See you soon." Erik leaned in for another kiss. "Call if you need me. I'll be right here."

After Ben left, Erik refilled his coffee and settled back in at the table. He started with hotel listings from the mid-nineties, around the time the Commodore Wilson was destroyed, and then went back decade by decade to identify hotels and other buildings that might have been a hiding place for the dome.

As the hours ticked by, Erik got an education in Cape May's real estate market as well as its rising and falling fortunes. At the time of the Commodore Wilson's destruction, the city wasn't as vibrant as it became later. During that slump, many older commercial properties and hotels fell onto hard times. Some were purchased and leveled, while others got a second wind.

A small number of locations just stopped being mentioned. Erik couldn't find a record of them being demolished, or any information about being sold or repurposed. If they fell into receivership, the proceedings dragged on for years without a published resolution. It didn't seem possible for the properties to just fall between the cracks, but it looked like that was exactly what happened.

By lunchtime, Erik had a list of a dozen possibilities. After a sandwich and soda, he whittled that down to five likely locations. Since Ben was busy with the rentals and wouldn't be able to run the leads on his computer until evening, Erik reached out to Brent Lawson, a friend who was also a private investigator.

"Erik, great to hear from you. To what potentially world-ending catastrophe do I owe the honor?" Brent greeted him.

"Who says there has to be an apocalypse for me to call?" Erik bantered.

"Because you don't usually want to talk about the latest blockbuster movie," Brent replied. "What's up?"

Brent lived in Pittsburgh and had a law enforcement background similar to Ben's. He often collaborated with them on problems involving magic and the supernatural, so Erik didn't have to worry about being believed. Brent even had experience dealing with the Pittsburgh Mob, so he understood that part of the equation.

"Old Mafia trouble, missing artwork, same old, same old."

"How can I help?"

"I need to run a couple of addresses for a history, and Ben's tied up with work. I'm hoping you can please do me a favor and put them through your databases."

"Yeah, sure. Not a problem. Ben's managed not to go back into the business?" Brent asked as Erik typed an email with the locations he was hoping to learn more about.

"He doesn't take new clients," Erik replied. "Technically, he's taking over the rental real estate business for his aunt and uncle, but he keeps his P.I. license so he can get the insider scoop when we get trouble. He's out all day, and I'm trying to make headway on some research that's pretty time-dependent."

Erik heard a ping on the other end of the connection.

"Got your email. Give me an hour or so, and I'll send you what I can get out of the databases. When are you and Ben going to come visit Pittsburgh?"

"I could ask when you're going to come up to Cape May. Bring Travis. We can go ghost hunting," Erik joked. Travis was Brent's work partner, and together they teamed up to stop supernatural dangers in Pittsburgh.

"Spring," Brent replied. "It's already getting cold here, and you're farther north."

"Fair enough. Let me know when you've got something. Thanks so much. I owe you."

Erik spent the next hour catching up on paperwork for the shop, dusting the displays, and ordering supplies. By the time Brent's email came through, he felt like he had managed to put in a good morning's work.

He texted Brent his thanks and dug into the trove of reports his friend sent. Brent's detective license and connections gave him access to data that was not openly available to the public, and the additional information helped Erik narrow his search.

After he waded through all the documents, Erik had a top contender, Weston Hall.

Named for an English country house and built in 1910, Weston Hall's builder had envisioned it as a grand manor befitting his fortune. He barely outlived the construction and left one heir, who died on the *Titanic*. The property sold to a developer who made it into a resort, which held its own until competition from other historic hotels siphoned off its clientele during Cape May's revitalization.

From there, Weston Hall passed through various hands, and its owners attempted a number of different ways to reinvent the buildings, from private school to conference center to hotel again. Age and upkeep made it increasingly expensive to maintain, and the parade of owners meant damage occurred as maintenance became irregular. Notably, it had a sizeable warehouse among its outbuildings.

By the time Thomas Bartolo bought Weston Hall in 1995, it had become something of a white elephant in the local real estate market. Bartolo's success and wealth from trucking and real estate came with ties to organized crime, and he was linked to the shady dealings of the firebrand preacher who was the Commodore Wilson's final owner.

Erik recognized Bartolo's name from the list he had compiled of people who made purchases at the Commodore Wilson's liquidation sale. He checked that information and confirmed that Bartolo had spent big money to purchase many of the doomed hotel's architectural features.

The liquidation sale records were spotty in places, but what Erik could find reported that Bartolo had his purchases shipped to his various properties, presumably to install them there. Erik didn't see a mention of Weston Hall, but it seemed likely that the most local property would receive some of the Commodore Wilson's pieces, for nostalgia value.

Whatever Bartolo's plans might have been, he was killed over a poker debt with another mobster. Lawyers and bankers litigated his estate, with claims and countersuits wending through the courts for years. Through it all, Weston Hall seemed forgotten, even as other properties found buyers.

According to the database information, Weston Hall remained abandoned and dilapidated, still tangled up in lawsuits. Its uncertain ownership and lack of a clear title, as well as unpaid debts, meant no one had been able to purchase the old hotel either to renovate it or tear it down for the land.

"Bingo," Erik muttered under his breath. That sounded like the perfect place for the dome's crates to go missing, overlooked in the storage area of a deserted ruin.

Curious about what Weston Hall had looked like in its glory days, Erik turned to the internet. He found photos of the building over the years of its checkered existence, as well as its long-ago British namesake.

The Cape May version of Weston Hall bore only a passing resemblance to its English cousin, an odd combination of British estate with elements from Cape May's Victorian and Edwardian opulence.

When Erik saw that Weston Hall had a narrow Tiffany-style arch over a main hallway, he felt certain he had found where the Commodore Wilson's dome had been languishing all these years.

Bartolo probably intended to install the dome to build on the archway Weston Hall already had. But what if he sent it there and then didn't live long enough to do anything with it?

Boxed in crates, the dome could easily be forgotten in the warehouse as the Weston became abandoned. No one would have known to look for it, and with the building left empty, the odds of being discovered by accident were slim. Erik hoped vandals hadn't happened upon it, but the heavy crates might have seemed too boring to attract attention.

The more he thought about it, the more convinced Erik became that Weston Hall was a likely resting place for the missing dome. When he searched online for photographs, he found relatively recent drone footage that showed the warehouse behind the main building covered with vegetation, nearly invisible behind an overgrown lawn with a sagging chain-link fence to keep out trespassers.

Erik couldn't wait to tell Ben about Weston Hall, but his call went to voicemail. Outside, the storm had grown worse, with the rain spattering against the windows in fat droplets, hitting hard enough it sounded like they could break the glass. Erik guessed that Ben had his hands full dealing with his property inspections and didn't envy him the drive home.

A crack of thunder made Erik jump. Then the lights went out.

"Shit." Erik took his laptop upstairs and got out enough candles to light the kitchen, glad that a gas stove meant he could at least make a hot dinner.

His phone rang, and he answered automatically, expecting a return call from Ben.

"We have him," a gravelly voice said. "And if you want him back, you will follow my instructions exactly."

SIX

BEN

"I'm cold, annoyed, and soaked to my skivvies," Ben grumbled as he unlocked the next-to-last of the houses he and his assistant were checking. The ones he'd thought likely to have problems, he'd already inspected with his maintenance crew. It was off-season, so more of the rentals were unoccupied than during the summer, when tenants usually called to report problems. The week of heavy rain and high winds made leaks and damage that much more likely.

"We've been lucky that the damage is minimal," Jenny replied. She had gone with him to help catalog what would need to be repaired. "We've had worse with other storms."

They wore hooded rain slickers to avoid dealing with umbrellas as they went in and out of houses, but at this point their coats were too wet to be fully water-repellent. Cold rain soaked Ben's face and ran down his neck. Good boots kept his feet warm and dry, but the rest of him felt cold and clammy.

"One more left after this," Ben remarked. They made quick work checking for the most common areas for storm damage. The house had been cleaned since the last tenant, but a dog collar lay on the counter with a dangling license, name tag, and tracker.

"We should probably call and see if they want this back," Ben said as he peered at the information on the license. He shoved the collar in his back pocket. "I'll do it tomorrow."

"Do you mind handling the last house?" Jenny asked when they reached the door. "I'm supposed to call a prospective renter at four, and the paperwork is back at the office."

"Go ahead," Ben said. "I figured I'll head home after I'm done. I'll type up the damage report, and we can deal with that tomorrow."

He waved as she got in her car, then crossed the street to the last rental house on the list. It was a cute cottage painted light blue with white filigree trim, not as large or fancy as some of the neighboring houses, but just right for a single renter or couple to spend a few months near the beach.

Mindful of Erik's warnings that morning, Ben sized up the area, taking in parked cars and looking for anyone who didn't belong. He had his pistol under his slicker, something he didn't usually feel the need to carry, since Cape May had a low crime rate, especially during the quiet season.

He couldn't help feeling jumpy, but nothing struck him as dangerous, and Ben chalked it up to cop nerves, a common side effect of hypervigilance.

Ben let himself into the house and locked the door behind him. He left his dripping slicker on the welcome mat and switched on the lights. They had done the outside checks on the property the previous day, leaving it to today to check inside the houses for evidence of leaks or water damage.

He headed to the second floor to check the small attic first. Nothing looked amiss, but Ben still couldn't shake the sense that something was wrong. He heeded his intuition and came downstairs with his gun in hand, sheepish when he faced an empty hallway.

Outside, thunder shook the house, and a flash of lightning lit up the sky through the windows. Ben couldn't wait to get home and find out what Erik had learned from his research.

He checked the bedrooms, making sure no water had gotten in around the windows. Ben tensed at an eerie whistling sound, and relaxed when he realized it was just the wind whipping around the house.

As he reached the bottom of the stairs, a brilliant streak of lightning and a loud burst of thunder made him jump.

The lights went out.

Ben froze, not because of the sudden darkness, but because he picked up the faint scent of aftershave that hadn't been present when he entered.

"Stop right there, Nolan. Put down the gun, and then put your hands in the air," a voice commanded.

The glow of a cell phone revealed three armed goons facing him, weapons drawn. Outnumbered and in the dark, Ben's odds in a fight were slim.

"What do you want?" He lowered his gun but didn't let go of the weapon.

"Put the gun on the floor and push it over to us."

Ben didn't recognize the speaker, but his heavy Jersey accent told him these were likely Newark Mob goons, not Russian Bratva.

He complied and straightened slowly with his hands in the air. "You're making a big mistake."

The speaker laughed. "Yeah, yeah. We know all about your boyfriend, the spy. If he gives us what we want, no one needs to get hurt."

Ben didn't believe that, but he wasn't going to argue.

The leader dialed a number, and Ben heard Erik answer. "We have him. And if you want him back, follow my instructions exactly."

Ben felt ice slither through his veins. He knew how the call would affect Erik, but with two guns trained on him, he didn't dare interfere.

"You have the Wildwood window," the leader said to Erik. "And we think you know where the big dome from that old hotel is. Give them to us, and your boyfriend walks away from here. I'll text you the location of the meeting spot."

The leader put his phone back in his pocket. Two men kept guns trained on Ben at close range while the leader pulled Ben's arms behind him and zip-tied his wrists. Ben's phone was in the pocket of his rain jacket, which hung near the front door.

"I hope Mitchell is a sensible fellow, and that he cares about you more than the stained glass," the leader said. "And in case you're wondering, the phone is a burner with location tracking spoofed. He's going to have to play by our rules to save you."

Ben didn't doubt that Erik would put his safety first, not just over the haunted window but over the dome, assuming he knew where it was. He doubted the mobsters would believe that Erik didn't have the dome and didn't know where it was; that didn't bode well.

Another clap of thunder and streak of lightning gave Ben a second look at his attackers. Three toughs, all in their late twenties, foot soldiers, not generals. They had been sent to fetch him and lay down the ultimatum, but they weren't the ones in charge.

"Did Barone put you up to this?" Ben asked as the leader hustled him toward the door.

"What do you care?"

"I keep track of who kidnaps me," Ben deadpanned.

Despite his earlier bravado, Ben knew Erik would be going insane with worry and felt certain he was already planning a rescue.

They went out the back door, Ben frog-marched between two of the goons. His captors cursed, scanning the area around them. A body lay sprawled in the yard, covered in blood, and Ben realized that the mobsters' lookout had been murdered.

That meant a second threat. Ben dropped to the ground, trying to stay out of the way as gunfire sounded and the Newark goons exchanged fire with a new enemy who had taken cover outside the door.

They didn't stand a chance. Within seconds, the Newark leader and his men sprawled dead on the concrete steps as a man in tactical gear with night vision goggles strode up and hauled Ben to his feet, giving him a quick once over.

Two others took Ben and held him up like a prize trophy as the new man in charge took a picture, then dialed a cell phone.

"Mitchell. Give us what we want, and no one dies." The Russian's accent didn't leave any question about his affiliation.

Ben heard the *zing* of a photo being sent. He couldn't make out Erik's response and wondered what his partner thought about the switch in kidnappers.

"The window from the Wildwood collector, and the dome from the Commodore Wilson. You'll find out where he is when we get what we want," the Russian replied to whatever Erik had said. "Keep the cops out of it, or I shoot him." He ended the call and spared Ben a disdainful glance. "Let's go."

The Jersey guys had taken Ben's gun, and the Russians didn't seem worried enough about what else he might be carrying to pat him down. They hurried him to a panel van parked behind the rental house and shoved him inside, driving away before the doors were closed.

Ben hoped the neighbors would report shots fired. Several of the nearby houses were occupied year-round. He hated to think of what the aftermath would look like for the cops to clean up. Moments later, he heard sirens and felt a flash of hope.

"You think Barone is going to accept killing his people and not come after you?" Ben asked from where he was sandwiched between two brawny men. "He wants the same windows."

"Shut up," the operative next to Ben growled and elbowed him hard in the ribs.

"Barone couldn't find his dick with both hands." The Russian drove with his headlights out through the dark streets at a speed that made Ben fear a whole different cause of death. "He is an idiot."

Ben didn't argue. The guard next to him had jammed the muzzle of his handgun into Ben's side, and point-blank, he couldn't miss. He and Erik had both been kidnapped more than Ben wanted to recall, and it never got less terrifying.

Ben tried to settle into his seat and felt a hard knot in his back pocket.

The dog collar had a tracker. Maybe Erik can use that to find me.

If Jenny remembers to mention it. If Erik can get in touch with the renters to have them track the tag. If the dog owners aren't too far out of range to pick up the signal.

That had better not be my only chance, or I'm royally screwed.

The sound of sirens faded. Occasional flashes of lightning lit up enough for Ben to realize they were heading out of town, toward the port. That made sense, since the commercial fishing hub had plenty of big warehouses, some of which were less active in the Fall. Even if Erik suspected that was where the Russians took him, finding them would take far too long.

"Get out." One of the goons dragged Ben from the van, and he nearly fell. The two men caught him and marched him inside at gunpoint.

Inside, a few security lights kept the warehouse from being completely dark, and Ben could hear the hum of a generator.

The smell of fish and industrial cleaner warred with each other. Outside, the storm still raged, and they were close enough to the ocean for the sound of the waves crashing on the seawall to rise above the thunder.

Ben remembered his hostage training, but the darkness made it difficult to see his surroundings, and his captors wore black neck gaiters pulled up to hide the lower half of their faces. He listened as they talked to each other in Russian and wondered what they were saying.

One of them disappeared into the shadows and returned after a time with a metal chair and a length of heavy rope, stained with fluids Ben didn't want to think about too hard.

"Sit." The man closest to Ben shoved him, and Ben fell more than sat. A second goon wrapped the rope tightly around Ben's chest. From the way he moved, Ben could tell the guy had plenty of practice. The Newark Mob were stone-cold killers, but the Russians brought a whole different level of lethality to the game.

"And now, we wait for Mitchell to do the sensible thing," one of the men said.

The Russians stayed in sight of Ben, but one found a table and another pulled out a deck of cards and some dice. Ben couldn't understand their conversation, but the tone and gestures reminded him of soldiers passing the time on a boring assignment.

Ben felt a chill and sensed that the warehouse ghosts had awakened. The Russians didn't seem to notice, or maybe they just didn't care. Some of the spirits hovered in the shadows around the edge of the large room, while others didn't—or couldn't—make themselves visible to Ben. He couldn't usually communicate with the ghosts, but an idea struck him, and he decided to try his luck.

"Warehouse ghosts. I can see you, and I need your help," he whispered, hoping his kidnappers would think he was praying, and hoping that the spirits would hear him and bother to assist.

"If you can leave this place, I need you to tell my friends where I am." Ben told them where to find Monty and Haley.

"These guys are mobsters. They're going to kill me unless you tell my friends where to find me." He thanked the ghosts and offered to return with a medium who could help them pass over.

Ben forced down his fear and let his training take over. He carefully scanned what he could see of the darkened warehouse, looking for anything that might work in his favor. That included memorizing the faces of his captors, now that they had removed their masks.

The few portable lights barely illuminated the center of the space. That made it easier to hide if he got loose, but gave him no idea of what might be hidden in the shadows. Equipment could shield him from pursuers or be an obstacle to his escape. Wires, cords, and pipes posed hazards if he needed to run.

Ben couldn't see far enough in the semi-darkness to spot any other exits aside from the door where they had entered. That meant running in any other direction could leave him trapped with no way out. If the warehouse had a security system, it was clearly deactivated. He wasn't very familiar with the port area, but there was little reason for traffic here, especially during the storm. No one was likely to notice unusual activity and call the police.

I won't allow them to use me as a bargaining chip with Erik. They'll kill both of us. No one is going to find me here, so I guess I'm going to need to figure out how to save myself.

He took inventory of what he could use. The goons hadn't patted him down since his gun was gone, so they didn't notice his pocketknife or the dog collar with the tracker. Ben had a key ring with several keys, but his phone was in his slicker, which got left at the rental house. His pen and notebook were also there.

Ben had remembered to inflate his chest before they wrapped the rope around him, but that didn't get him enough wiggle room to get free, and his captors could see his every move. The metal chair wouldn't break easily, and while they hadn't tied his ankles, he wasn't going to get far in the dark. He might be able to stand up and smack someone with the chair, although that wouldn't deter men with weapons for long.

But several feet to his left, Ben spotted a large pile of boxes. If they weren't too heavy, he might be able to get to the stack and knock it over if a diversion was needed. It wouldn't hold back the mobsters for long, but it might slow them down for a few seconds.

The same darkness that kept Ben from seeing more of the warehouse would make pursuit difficult, unless the mobsters had flashlights that they hadn't used yet.

Time dragged. Ben had no idea how long it had been since he'd been brought in, but he guessed a couple of hours had passed. Outside, the wind rattled loose sheet-metal panels, and the thunder echoed. Somewhere in the shadows, water dripped with a relentless patter. Lightning streaks glowed through windows high up on the walls, but otherwise, the lack of light told Ben it was still night.

Ben tried to remain alert for an opportunity. He reminded himself that circumstances could change suddenly and that he might still find a way to escape, or at least put up a good fight.

The leader called Erik a second time, telling him to bring the haunted stained-glass window and the location of the Tiffany dome to a parking lot near the port at dawn. That didn't reveal much about where Ben was imprisoned, since it was a large area with hundreds of hiding places. He didn't have any faith that the Russians would let him and Erik walk away, even if Erik met their demands. The two of them had been too effective at stopping both Bratva and the Newark Mafia too many times for them to be set free.

I don't see a way out.

Ben wasn't giving up, but the odds weren't in his favor.

I just moved in with Erik, and it was going so well. We're a good match, better than I ever thought I'd find. He's everything I ever wanted in a partner, and for the first time in a long while, I've been happy.

When Ben made the move to Cape May, he wasn't sure he'd find his footing or ever fall in love again. Rental real estate was a long way from being a cop or a detective. That was the point, plus taking over the rental company, but it really seemed like a long shot.

To Ben's surprise, he found himself liking a job that wasn't one emergency after another, and realized that he was good at it. Returning to the town brought back fond memories of spending summers helping his aunt and uncle when he was a teenager. Cape May, which he had feared would seem dreadfully dull after the big city had grown on him. Of course, the supernatural dangers he and Erik fought were anything but dull.

Most of all, he'd met Erik when Ben had nearly given up finding a forever match. And now their time was being cut short.

I'll fight to keep what we have with everything I've got, but we might have run out of luck this time.

I hope Erik knows how much I love him, how much I cherish the time we've had together. If this is all we get, it's better than none at all.

But damn, I wanted to get old and gray and totter into the sunset together. We never even had a chance to get a dog.

If I don't make it, it'll throw a wrench into my aunt and uncle's retirement. I was their way out. Will they find someone else to buy the business, or have to sell off the properties piecemeal? That'll play havoc with their plans.

With the power out, I wonder how long it'll take the police to find those bodies on the steps at the other house. Hendricks will have a heart attack over that. Jenny will worry herself sick over me.

And being the scene of a Mob hit isn't going to do good things for attracting new renters.

Not to mention that Erik and I might not be around to do our programs for the festival. I wonder if new attacks will make the organizers decide to cancel, just to be safe. That would be a shame. People put in a lot of work. One more thing I was looking forward to.

Ben shook off the mood. *Feeling sorry for myself isn't going to change anything. Either we'll live through this or we won't.*

But it sure would be great to take some of these sons of bitches out with us. Screw up their plans, keep the Tiffany windows out of their boss's hands, make this an expensive failure for them.

In the absence of hope, Ben decided vengeance would do.

SEVEN

ERIK

E rik stared at his phone, unable to breathe. The mobster's threat chilled him to the bone, and he feared for Ben's life.

It took a couple of moments to control his breathing and let his heartbeat slow so he could think.

New Jersey accent, so that's Newark Mafia. They must have grabbed him at one of the rental houses. Where would they take him, and how do I get him back safely?

The reality of the threat had barely sunk in when his phone rang again. Erik answered, expecting the first caller to set out the terms of trading the windows for Ben.

Instead, a new voice with a thick Russian accent spoke. "Mitchell. Give us what we want, and no one dies." A photo of Ben held captive between two masked toughs made it clear that there had been some kind of dangerous hand-off.

"Who is this? What do you want?" Erik's training kicked in even though his heart thudded and his mind spun at this new twist. The Newark Mob didn't cooperate with Bratva. Whatever had changed didn't bode well for Ben's safety.

"The window from the Wildwood collector, and the dome from the Commodore Wilson. You'll find out where he is when we get what we want," the Russian replied. "Keep the cops out of it, or I shoot him." He ended the call.

"Shit, shit, shit." Erik reminded himself not to grip his phone so hard that it cracked.

He tried to get a location on the number that called him and wasn't surprised that tracking had been disabled. Bratva was a dangerous criminal organization, professionals on a different level than the Newark mobsters.

The power was still out, so Hendricks and his officers would be busy dealing with the storm's effects. Without more details, there was nothing Erik could tell the police that was worth the risk of making contact.

His phone rang, and Haley's number came up.

"Erik? What's going on? I just had a couple of ghosts show up and say that Ben sent them to me because he's been kidnapped," Haley told him.

"Yes. Did they tell you anything?" Erik wasn't ashamed of the desperation in his voice.

"They're Russian, and they have him in a warehouse on the waterfront," Haley reported. "Ben told them to make sure you know he loves you."

Erik consciously slowed his breathing, trying not to hyperventilate. "Okay. That's more than I knew before. Did they give you more details about which warehouse?"

"No. Ghosts aren't usually good at that sort of thing," Haley replied. "Sorry."

"Don't apologize," Erik told her. "We know Ben's still alive and that his kidnappers haven't left the city. They haven't told me where the drop is, but I'm going to guess it's not too far from where they're holding Ben."

"Don't trust them," Haley warned.

"Don't worry," Erik said with a bitter laugh. "I won't. Please let me know if you hear from the ghosts again."

"I will," she promised. "I tried to ask them questions, but they didn't answer. But I'll keep the channel open."

Erik thanked her and called Alessia, cursing under his breath until she picked up. "I need your help." He knew he sounded panicked.

"Erik? What's wrong?"

"Bratva kidnapped Ben." He was still trying not to hyperventilate. Erik knew he needed all his experience to get Ben back, but he couldn't completely shut down the fear that coursed through him.

"How?"

"I don't know what happened, but first the New Jersey Mob claimed that they had him, and then not long afterward, a Russian called me back."

"Are you sure it's true?"

"They sent me a picture." Erik did his best to wall up his feelings, needing to focus on a strategy to outwit the kidnappers and save Ben. "Then a ghost told Haley that Ben's being held in a warehouse, but didn't have specifics."

"I'm so sorry," Alessia replied. "How can I help?"

He gave her a quick outline of the situation, including the window, the dome, and the interest of The Collector and The Oligarch. "The two men at the top are witches, but I doubt they came in person to grab Ben," he added. "I'd be surprised if they brought in fighters with supernatural abilities. Too much temptation for them to use those talents against the boss."

"Makes sense," Alessia agreed.

"I was hoping you could do a tracking spell on Ben. Having the power out makes normal recon nearly impossible."

"Have you called the police?"

"Not yet. The kidnappers told me not to tell the cops. And until I know for certain where he's being held, there's nothing the police can do. I don't believe that the guys who took him will hand Ben over and let us both walk out of there, even if I give them what they want," Erik said.

"True," Alessia agreed. "As for the cops, it doesn't count if I call Cole, and it keeps you out of hot water with the chief for not keeping him informed," she added in a sly tone.

"I can't match the Mafia for firepower, and Ben's likely to get hurt in the fighting if we go in guns blazing. But if we can use magic and ghosts, we might stand a chance."

"I'm in," Alessia said. "I'll scry for Ben. Having Haley ask the ghosts for help is a good idea. They don't care that it's storming and the lights are out."

"Thank you." Erik could hear the strain in his voice. "I'll let you know if I find out anything."

"Same here. Good luck. And I'll send some protective spells Ben's way," she promised before disconnecting.

Haley's number showed up as soon as the call ended. "I've got more intel from the ghost," she told him.

"What did he have to say?" Erik was desperate for any clues that might help them bring Ben back alive.

"He gave me a description of a warehouse in the port where Ben's being held. Used to be Sanderson Seafood. The cops will be able to find it," Haley said. "The ghost said there are at least three guards, sometimes more, and that the warehouse is haunted and the other spirits will help us. How do you want to play this?"

"Alessia was going to scry for Ben and is working protective magic. She's all in for helping get Ben back," Erik told Haley. "Since the warehouse is haunted, maybe you can come up with a plan so the ghosts can lend a hand?"

"I can do that," Haley said. "And I'll call Father Dennis, just in case they're working with any darker entities. Magic and guns are bad enough, but it can't hurt to be over-prepared."

"Thank you. Let's reconnect in half an hour." Erik realized after he ended the call that he was still standing with the phone in his hand, frozen in place. He went back to the kitchen and gathered what he needed.

Erik lit a candle and smudged with sage, then put a salt circle around his chair. He mixed dried mugwort, rosemary, and tobacco in a shallow bowl and lit it, letting the smoke mingle with the sage.

Deep breaths helped him get settled, and he pictured Ben clearly in his mind.

Help me save him, Erik sent out to the universe. *I need to save him.*

Erik couldn't be sure that ghosts or the cosmos heard him, but the ritual calmed him and helped to clear his thoughts.

A power brick kept his phone at full charge despite the continued outage. He searched on the name the ghost had given Haley and found a picture of a run-down warehouse along with an address.

More than we knew before, but we need a plan. Where to park, how to approach, how to get inside. We can't afford to fuck this up.

His phone rang again, this time from the number the Russian had used.

"Mitchell. Bring the Wildwood window and the location of the Tiffany dome and meet us in two hours." He gave an address, which Erik hurriedly wrote down. "No cops."

"What about Ben? Hostage exchange, Ben for the windows."

"We will tell you where he's being held once you deliver the goods," the caller said. "All in good faith."

His response confirmed Erik's suspicion that the Russians never meant to let either of them go. Without the ghost's message, Erik would have feared that Ben was already dead. Once Bratva had what they wanted, they had no reason to allow either Ben or Erik to live.

"All right," Erik agreed, already making a plan.

"Come alone. Follow instructions, and this will be simple."

As simple as walking right into a trap.

"Two hours. Starting now." The Russian ended the call.

Before Erik could call Alessia or Haley, his phone rang yet again, the caller tagged as the Cape May Chief of Police.

"Mitchell. Alessia called me about Ben being kidnapped. There are three dead mobsters at a Nolan rental house. What do you know?" Hendricks's gravelly voice suggested he had spent most of the day out in the storm.

"They're Newark Mob," Erik said. "They kidnapped Ben, then got jumped by Bratva. The Russians took Ben and want me to give them the stained-glass window in exchange."

"Jesus, Mitchell. How do you know who the dead guys were?"

"Because they called me to extort a trade, and then the Russians called me right after. Since those two groups don't play nicely together, I figured that Bratva got the drop on the Jersey guys and took Ben."

"Do you trust them to exchange Ben for the window?" Hendricks asked.

"Hell no. They'll kill both of us. We've gotten in their way too many times."

"Did they give you a meeting place?"

Ben's only chance to survive would be if Erik, Alessia, and Haley could rescue him before the rendezvous. Once Ben was safe, Erik had no reason not to bring in the police.

"Yeah, write this down." Erik gave the address and the time. "I don't know how many goons there are, and they'll be armed. The leader said Ben would be kept at a second location until I make the handoff. I'm positive it's a trap."

"No shit," Hendricks muttered. "You're the Mob expert, and it's your partner's life on the line. What's your plan?"

"A ghost told us the area where Ben's being held. A couple friends and I are going to use ghosts and magic to rescue Ben. We can't win a shootout, so this is Ben's only chance. Once Ben's safe, your team shows up at the rendezvous site to take out the trash."

Erik held his breath, waiting for Hendricks's response.

"Ghosts and magic? You're sure enough to bet Ben's life on that?"

"You know I wouldn't risk it if I weren't," Erik replied.

"These friends agreed? How do you know these Mafia guys don't have woo-woo of their own?"

"I don't know for certain, but I'm pretty sure," Erik admitted. "Both The Collector and The Oligarch are witches in their own right, but they wouldn't come themselves, they'd send underlings. Witches are pretty careful about not having other people with abilities working for them. It increases the chance for betrayal."

"There'll be hell to pay if you're wrong," Hendricks warned.

"I'm well aware." Left unsaid was that if this all went sideways, he and Ben wouldn't be around for the aftermath.

"Okay. I'll back your play. Because I think you're right. If we move on where Ben's being held, they'll kill him before we can stop them," Hendricks said. "Doesn't mean I like it, but I agree. This time."

Erik quickly packed what he would need to help Haley summon the spirits and Alessia to work the necessary magic. For a magical working with so much at stake, they would have to sneak into where the kidnappers had Ben to rally the ghosts and have the magic work at full strength.

He called Haley and Alessia and caught them up on the second message from Bratva and his conversation with the chief.

"I understand if you want to do the magic from a distance," Erik said. "I wouldn't blame you. Sneaking inside is taking a crazy chance. I'll be grateful for any support you can provide, but I've got to go myself."

"I'm going with you," Alessia said without hesitating, and Haley echoed the same seconds later. "I'll get everything ready. Pick me up on your way."

Erik thanked them profusely and barely ended the call before his phone rang again from Ben's assistant.

"Erik, terrible things have happened, and I think Ben is in danger," Jenny said breathlessly.

"I know," he replied. "I talked to Chief Hendricks about the shooting victims, and Ben's been kidnapped."

"I was afraid of that," Jenny replied. "But I might be able to help. In the last house we visited together, the previous tenants had left behind a dog collar with a tracking tag. He stuck it in his pocket to see if they still wanted it.

"When the chief told me about the murders, I worried that they had taken Ben," she continued. "I called the renter and got them to check the location tag. It's still active. It's showing a warehouse at the port, and there's no reason for the collar to be there if it isn't still in Ben's pocket."

"You're absolutely brilliant." Erik reached for pen and paper. "Please read the address off to me." When it turned out to be exactly the same as the address provided by the ghost, he breathed a sigh of relief.

"I will let the chief know," he promised. "Good thinking. This will help us save him."

"I feel so guilty," Jenny confided. "I didn't go to the last house with him because I had something to do back in the office, and I keep thinking that maybe if he hadn't been alone, this wouldn't have happened."

Erik's heart went out to her, but he knew that things would have been much worse if she had been with Ben.

"Please don't feel guilty. The people who took him are professional criminals. They would have hurt you and still taken him. He wouldn't have wanted you mixed up in that."

"Bring him back safely," Jenny said.

"We will." Erik left a quick voicemail for the chief with the update about the dog tag, figuring that Hendricks would appreciate the validation from something other than a ghost. Erik took a moment to go online and study a street view of the warehouse and figure out where to park and how to approach the building so he, Alessia, and Haley wouldn't give themselves away.

Then he grabbed his duffel, holstered his gun, made sure he had plenty of ammo, and headed for Alessia's house.

We're coming, Ben. Hang in there. Please be safe. Come back to me alive.

The rain had let up some, but it made for miserable driving. The wet road reflected his headlights, and the power outage meant everything else was completely dark. The windshield wipers kept a steady beat, barely clearing enough water for him to see.

Alessia and Haley waited under the carport at Alessia's house. They put their bags in the back where Haley sat, while Alessia slid into the passenger seat for the drive to the warehouse. "Perfect night for a rescue, don't you think?" Haley said with forced bravery and a confident grin that didn't quite reach her eyes.

"At least it means there's almost no one out on the roads. Less chance to be spotted." Erik caught them up on the call from Jenny and what he had learned from his online reconnaissance.

"Turn the headlights off when we get close and try to stay away from any security lights that might still be working," Alessia told him.

"I've got a spell that won't exactly make us invisible, but it encourages people not to see us. I hope it will be enough."

Erik fervently agreed. He had never been very religious, but he sent up any prayers he remembered to whoever might be listening to protect them and help them get Ben home safely.

"I also brought deflection amulets for us." Alessia handed out chains with charms to Erik and Haley, who slipped them on. "Works the same way as the car spell. We won't be invisible, but we'll be easy to ignore."

He hoped the heavy rain would keep spotters to a minimum. Erik turned off the headlights two blocks from the warehouse and found a curbside spot to park.

"Ready? Still time to change your mind," he told Alessia and Haley.

"Born ready. Let's go get Ben," Alessia said.

They were soaked minutes after they left the car, but they had feared the crinkle and shuffle of raincoats more than the chill of the rain. Erik had night-vision goggles from his work with Interpol, and Alessia had a spell that sharpened her vision. Erik sensed that ghosts were nearby and wondered if they helped guide Haley through the gloom.

Just behind the warehouse, they stepped into an alley, and Haley concentrated on the ghosts.

"We'd sure appreciate any help from the ghosts in the warehouse," she whispered. "If you've wanted to kick ass, now's the time." She paused a moment. "The ghost Ben sent is here. He says the back door is unlocked and the other spirits are ready to rumble."

"Will the 'shit spell' that's on the store's front door work?" Erik asked, looking for a potent distraction and a way to disable the goons while minimizing gunfire.

Alessia concentrated for a moment, then shook her head. "No. I'm picking up flickers of magic. I think they're wearing protections against that sort of small-scale curse. But what they have won't be enough to stop what I've got in mind."

"Wait for us to get inside, and then give 'em hell," Erik murmured.

"There's no warding on the building, and I'm not picking up on anyone with magic inside," Alessia reported.

"But there are dozens of ghosts," Haley added.

Erik wondered whether the spirits were all from people who died in the warehouse or if their ghostly guide had recruited from the whole port area. He suspected a long history of dangerous conditions, injuries, and deaths led to the haunting and gave the ghosts good reason to be angry. Now they had a target and a mission and the power to make someone pay.

No matter where the ghosts came from, he was grateful for their help.

"Let's go." Erik gestured and together they headed inside. To his relief, the warehouse wasn't completely dark. A few portable lights illuminated a circle in the main area with the mobsters and their prisoner, leaving the sides of the massive, barn-like building in shadow.

Six men dressed like Bratva operatives sat around a small table. Nearby, Ben sat tied securely to a metal chair.

Alessia looked at Erik and nodded, confirming that she saw Ben.

Haley closed her eyes. "Go get 'em," she mouthed silently to the ghosts as Alessia began to work her magic to strengthen the spirits and weaken the mobsters' protections.

Erik, Haley, and Alessia positioned themselves out of sight behind pallets of boxes. They could still see between the pallets, and Erik hoped it would be sufficient protection from bullets and any retaliatory magic the thugs might muster.

A freezing cold wind rose out of nowhere and swept toward where the mobsters were playing cards, howling like the hounds of hell. The gusts came from all corners, echoing from steel and concrete.

"Jesus, what the fuck is going on?" The mobsters jumped to their feet, weapons drawn, looking around in a panic.

Haley chanted in a whisper, and the ghosts grew stronger. Alessia spoke words of power causing the shipping containers to tremble and make a terrible racket. Erik clenched his fists, ready to move. The spirits swept toward the Mob goons, gaping maws and grasping hands, screaming and screeching like the damned.

The Bratva boys raised their guns to shoot at the apparitions, but Alessia's magic jammed the weapons, making them useless.

Praying and swearing, the mobsters held up their protective amulets like shields against the ghosts, to no avail. Erik didn't understand all the Russian words the men yelled at the attackers, but he got enough to know they were alternately trying to banish the spirits and beg for their lives.

Meanwhile, Erik saw Ben hitching his chair away from the mobsters, putting distance between himself and them.

Summoned by Haley and empowered by Alessia's magic, the ghosts channeled their fury like a whirlwind. They buffeted the enforcers, shoving them so hard they stumbled, and upended their table, sending cards and dice flying.

Gray shapes with hollow-eyed faces stalked the mobsters. Bony hands grabbed and held those who tried to run.

Creaks, groans, and rattles sounded from the shadows as more ghosts gathered. Erik kept his eyes on Ben as he willed him to be okay.

Ben's chair tipped over, and he fell onto his side. Erik held his breath as he watched Ben push himself along, heading into the shadows. His captors were too overwhelmed by their ghostly tormentors to notice.

Ghosts clawed at the guards and ripped their clothing, tearing out hair and raising bloody welts on faces and arms. The mobster's top boss might be a witch, but these soldiers clearly had no ability with the supernatural and had not made any preparations to protect themselves from powerful paranormal threats.

Erik stifled a gasp as one of the ghosts tore out the throat of a Bratva operative, letting the body fall in a spray of blood. A spectral hand clawed across another mobster's eyes, blinding him with blood before the ghost reached into the man's ribcage and then dropped his corpse to the floor.

The four remaining Russians tried to fight the ghosts, who seemed to be toying with their victims. The spirits attacked from one direction and then another, scoring bloody slashes. One man fell to his knees, praying and begging. A ghost passed right through the supplicant, who stiffened and then fell face down, dead. Another man's neck suddenly twisted with an awful *crack,* and he tumbled to the floor.

The main door to the warehouse flew open, and six new mobsters charged in. Erik could see enough to know these weren't Bratva reinforcements. The Newark Mob had arrived to retaliate with a show of force.

"What the fuck?" The Newark goons' guns jammed, and as they took in the horrific scene in front of them, the ghosts turned their attention and ire on the newcomers.

A tide of ghosts encircled the men, cutting off retreat. The Newark men tried to bludgeon the spirits with their now-useless guns, but the revenants tore the weapons from their hands and threw them into the shadows. Whatever protective medallions they might have worn did them no good as the spirits closed ranks, enveloping the men in an undulating gray storm.

Voices screamed in English and Italian. Through the gauzy haze of ghostly forms, Erik saw the ghosts ripping the mobsters apart, and a growing pool of blood flowed across the concrete floor.

He hoped that Alessia and Haley could control the spirits, so they didn't become the next targets.

With the soldiers down, Erik darted out to drag Ben the rest of the way to safety and cut through his bonds. "Are you hurt?" He was unable to see much in the limited light.

"Roughed up a little, nothing serious," Ben told him.

"I'll be right behind you," Haley assured him. "Just making sure the ghosts get to have some fun."

Erik sent a pre-written text to Chief Hendricks.

Erik: *They're all yours. Ben is safe.*

"Let's get out of here," Erik said to Alessia and Haley. He couldn't tell if the ghosts had left any of the mobsters alive.

"Thank you," Haley told the ghosts. "Keep the bad guys down, but don't hurt the cops. I'll come back tomorrow and send anyone on who wants to go."

The spirits didn't acknowledge, but Erik felt sure they heard.

They were already in the SUV and a couple of blocks away by the time police cars streamed past them, sirens blaring and lights flashing. He wondered what Hendricks would make of the scene he was going to find and figured he would get the connection to the magical protection of Trinkets' security system once he saw the incapacitated mobsters.

"You came." Ben sat in the passenger seat, and Alessia was in the back with Haley and their gear. Erik blasted the heat since they were all soaked from the storm.

"Of course we came," Erik replied. "I'm damn glad you had that dog tag. It helped me convince Hendricks. But Haley's ghosts and Alessia's magic are the real heroes."

"Kudos all the way around," Alessia said, "but especially to the ghosts."

"Lucky for us, the ghosts were itching for some payback," Haley added.

Just as they reached Alessia's house, the streetlights lit up. "Perfect timing." Erik was glad that the darkness from the power outage had made Ben's rescue a little easier.

"Be careful," Alessia warned as she and Haley got out. Their clothing clung to their skin, and Erik figured he and Ben didn't look much better. She turned to Haley. "Why don't you stay over with me?"

"Sounds great," Haley agreed. "Safety in numbers."

"You got rid of the henchmen, but the bosses are still out there," Alessia reminded them. "If you need magic, just let me know."

"Same here," Haley assured them.

"I'm trying not to think about that right now," Erik admitted. "One problem at a time."

"Thank you," Ben said. "I owe you."

"Pfft. That's what friends do." Alessia said. She and Haley headed inside. Ben and Erik watched until they were sure the door was closed and the lights turned on.

"Do I need to take you to the Emergency Room?" Erik asked. There wasn't enough light in the car for him to get a good idea of whether Ben was seriously injured.

"No. Other than a few punches, they didn't even rough me up," Ben said. "I'll have some bruises, but it's nothing ice and ibuprofen can't handle, and I really don't want to deal with the paperwork and questions."

Even though the police were on their side this time, Erik knew that Ben's story would get all the wrong kind of attention. They couldn't afford to have the story leak to the media, and even though Cape May didn't have an aggressive press corps, any story with mafia connections got top coverage.

"Okay, for now. If anything changes, come up with a cover story, and I'll take you to see a doctor," Erik said.

Ben hesitated, then relented. "I'll let you know if I think that's necessary."

Erik knew that their previous jobs both came with a fair amount of physical danger and had a culture of pushing through the pain. Now that they were making their own rules, he was done with fore-going necessary treatment to look tough.

As soon as they were inside and the alarms were on, Erik turned Ben under the light so he could look for injuries.

"Erik, I'm all right." Ben had a look in his eyes that said he under-stood the desperate worry beneath the fussing.

Erik pulled Ben into a tight hug, wrapping his arms around him and burying his face in Ben's neck.

"I thought I was going to lose you," Erik confessed. "When Haley said your ghost friend showed up, I was afraid I already had. God, Ben, I was so scared."

"So was I." Ben made no move to free himself from Erik's arms. "I knew they intended to kill both of us, whether you brought the window or not. I couldn't get loose. I thought we might have finally run out of luck."

Erik pushed back enough to see the aftermath of emotions in his eyes. He kissed him long and deep, proof of life.

"You're soaking wet," Ben said, as if noticing for the first time.

"Price of admission tonight." Erik's voice came out rough. "Let's get you in the shower and changed out of those clothes. You smell like mobster."

"What is it with those guys and aftershave?" Ben replied in a shaky attempt at humor.

"Better than herring and onions, like Bratva," Erik quipped. "Come on. Let's go upstairs."

The shower wasn't quite big enough for both of them. Erik helped Ben undress, silently cataloging every bruise and scratch, then stripped down himself. He put extra towels on the floor and gently pushed Ben under the water once it was warm but not hot.

"Let me take care of you." He took his time soaping Ben's arms and torso for the excuse to run his hands all over, assuring him that his lover was safe and alive. He took special care with Ben's shoulders and upper arms, where he had been tied, expecting bruises the next day from the ropes.

The familiar herbal smell of shampoo and soap soothed both of them. Erik slicked his hands again and worked down over Ben's ass and legs, before reaching between for his taint and balls, then around to stroke his cock.

"Tell me what you want." Erik knew from experience that danger and its aftermath could either stoke hunger or kill desire.

"You, touching me. I want to feel you," Ben said. "I want to know we're both alive."

Erik leaned in to kiss Ben's shoulder. One hand wrapped around Ben's cock, and the other slipped between his legs. "Don't think. Just feel."

Ben thickened under his touch, and Erik felt himself get stiff, despite the night's emotional roller coaster. He doubted it would take long for either of them, but the release would help them both wind down.

Ben braced himself against the shower wall. Erik stepped closer and slotted his own prick between Ben's ass cheeks, not trying to penetrate but using them for friction as his strokes matched his hand's movement.

"Let go," he murmured. "Let it all go."

Ben shot hard against the tile wall. Erik came seconds later, painting Ben's back with white stripes. He clung to Ben for a moment until he was sure neither of them had gone weak in the knees, then soaped Ben down again and wiped off the wall.

"Let's get into dry clothes." Erik wrapped Ben in a towel and made sure they hadn't left puddles on the floor. Erik dried him and helped him into a soft T-shirt and sleep shorts before toweling off and grabbing a pair of soft flannel pants.

"You've missed a couple of meals," Erik pointed out. "Are you hungry? Or should I ask, can you eat?"

Ben shook his head. "I probably should, but I'm not sure anything would stay down right now, even water."

Erik felt the same way, even though he had forced himself to eat a sandwich earlier. "Okay. Let me know if you change your mind."

They made their way to the bedroom, and Erik drew Ben under the covers. Sated from the encounter in the shower and exhausted from the day, Erik was happy just to hold Ben close and listen to him breathe.

"I love you," Erik murmured, and Ben echoed his words. "Now, sleep."

Erik worried he might lie awake with racing thoughts of the ways the day could have gone wrong. He wouldn't be surprised if they woke with nightmares. But right now, warm and wrapped around his lover, Erik felt Ben relax into sleep and followed moments later.

———

The phone's shrill ring woke Erik. He reluctantly separated himself from where he had spooned around Ben and answered the call.

"Mitchell, how's Nolan?" Chief Hendricks's brusque tone was tempered with genuine concern.

"Remarkably unhurt." Erik cast a glance over his shoulder at his still-sleeping partner. "At least physically. That kind of thing stays with you in other ways for a long time."

Erik had survived shootouts and hostage situations before and knew the toll it took.

"Glad you're both okay," the chief said. "We got the guys who showed up to take the window for ransom. Only a couple of survivors from the warehouse. As for the pile of dead bodies, I'd understand gunshot wounds, but most of those guys looked like they'd been attacked by wild animals. Want to explain?"

"Would you believe me if I did?" Erik asked.

"You're going to say something like ghosts or magic, aren't you?" the chief replied in a resigned tone.

"Yep. Don't ask questions if you don't want to hear the answers," Erik said. "I went in with a witch and a medium. Those guys had a lot of enemies."

"I'd like to get the two of you down here to take a look at the survivors, and you should probably see if any of the bodies at the morgue look familiar," the chief added. "I'm going to ship them off to Newark once they can provide secure transport, but I figured Nolan could identify the guys who grabbed him, and you might recognize the Russians."

"Ben can probably ID more of them. I'd recognize the voice of the Russian who called me, but I never saw them except in the warehouse, and things were going crazy."

"That's good enough. Try to make it in the next hour or so. Then I can have someone take out the trash," Hendricks said.

Ben wandered into the kitchen as the call ended. "What's up?"

"Hendricks wants us to come down to the station and ID your kidnappers and the guys who extorted me for the window. Are you up for it?"

"They had their faces covered when they grabbed me, but later in the warehouse, when they were playing cards, they got careless. I'm pretty sure I can. And they were Russian. That sort of narrows down the choices," Ben replied.

"We've got an hour or so," Erik told him. "Get dressed. Take another shower if you want. I'll fix breakfast."

Ben shot him a thumbs-up and wandered toward the bedroom. Erik heard the shower turn on and knew that part of getting over an ordeal like Ben had experienced involved washing away the feeling of contamination left behind by the kidnappers. It wasn't logical, but it was very real.

He started a fresh pot of coffee, stuck bread in the toaster, and made fried eggs, usually a weekend treat. By the time Ben came back to the kitchen, breakfast was ready.

"This looks fantastic," Ben told him. "Thank you, I'm starving. I think my body realized I survived. Last night, I wasn't completely sure."

Erik stood behind him and leaned down to hug him. "I'm just glad you're here. Do you need ibuprofen? Change your mind about going to the ER?"

Ben shook his head. "Considering everything, I'm actually in pretty good shape. A few new bruises, but no blood. Thanks for checking."

They dug into the food, intent on polishing it off while everything was still hot. Ben gulped down coffee, and Erik brought the carafe over for refills. When they were finished, Ben looked up.

"So…the cops. What does Hendricks know?"

"Almost everything," Erik replied. "He knows about the window and the dome, and that Newark and Bratva fought over them. He even knows about the magic and the ghosts. I was surprised he went along with it. Susan must be having an impact on him."

"Hendricks is level-headed. If he'd have tried to go in there with a SWAT team, we'd have had an even bigger blood bath," Ben answered. "Does Cape May even *have* a SWAT team?"

"Actually, yes," Erik said. "But I'm pretty sure that was the conclusion he came to as well. Plus, he's done enough clean-up after our cases to believe in the supernatural…at least a little."

"What about after we're done with the cops?" Ben asked. "Do you really know where the Tiffany dome is?"

"Pretty sure I do." Erik set his coffee cup aside and filled Ben in on the research he had done on Weston Hall and its unlucky former owner.

"I called Cassidy while you were still sleeping, and she said Sorren, Archibald Donnelly, and Rowan would be here after sundown to retrieve both the haunted stained glass and the dome if it's where I think it is."

Donnelly, a powerful necromancer, often worked with Cassidy and Sorren on dangerous supernatural cases, as did Rowan, a very talented witch.

"You think the dome is still crated up?" Ben asked.

"Weston Hall is the most likely place I've been able to identify," Erik said. "Bartolo bought a lot of architectural items when the Commodore Wilson did its liquidation sale and shipped them out. It would be easy for people to overlook a couple more crates that weren't on the manifest.

"Then he got killed, and there was no one to follow up or know where to look for the dome. Alessia thinks there may be spells involved, too, keeping the dome hidden. Weston Hall pretty much went to hell after that, so no one looked too closely at what was inside its warehouse because the property wasn't sold or remodeled," Erik recapped.

"Makes sense to me. What will Sorren do with it?" Ben asked.

"Pass it off to the Briggs Society or the Alliance, like usual. No one will ever see the windows again, and they won't cause any more danger." Erik felt relieved that once they made the handoff, he no longer had responsibility for the dangerous stained glass.

"Good riddance. I'll be glad to get that thing out of the safe and out of here." Ben drained the last of his coffee. "Same for the dome. But will the bad guys ever believe you don't have them?"

"I was prepared to hand all of it over to Bratva if I believed that would buy your safety," Erik admitted. "But I've gone up against those sons of bitches before, and I knew they were lying about letting you go."

"Thank you," Ben said quietly, looking down at his cup. "For everything. Being willing to turn those over to save me, and mounting the most awesome rescue ever."

"I love you." Erik thought that explained everything. "That's what you do when you're in love."

Putting off the meeting with the cops wouldn't change anything, so Erik and Ben reluctantly rinsed the dishes and headed for the station.

"Mitchell, Nolan, glad you're in one piece," Hendricks greeted them when they arrived. "Thanks for coming. I can take you to the cell block, or if you'd prefer they not see your faces, we can put them in the interview room with one-way glass."

"Pretty sure they already know who we are," Erik replied in a dry voice.

"Do you need to alert Interpol or MI6 or someone?"

Erik had thought about that overnight and came to a conclusion. "I don't think so. They came for the window and the Tiffany dome. Finding out Ben and I were involved was unexpected. They weren't originally after us. I figure you're turning them over to the FBI to deal with."

Hendricks grunted in agreement. "Yeah, and I'm hoping the Feds can keep them from coming back. Although I doubt we'll get that lucky."

Given the long-standing Mafia ties with the Commodore Wilson and other properties in town, Erik knew Hendricks couldn't really blame him and Ben for attracting criminals to the area.

"They've seen us. Just take us to the cells." Ben squared his shoulders and stood a little taller. Erik knew his partner was mustering courage to face his captors and loved him even more for it.

Hendricks led them to the back, and an officer unlocked the door to the holding cells. Three mobsters looked up when they entered. One was heavily bandaged, and his stricken expression suggested that the ghostly attack inflicted mental trauma as well as physical injuries.

"These are the survivors," Hendricks said. "The bodies from the attack at the rental house and the guys from whatever-the-hell happened at the warehouse are at the morgue. Two of them we arrested after Erik got you out of the warehouse, part of the Newark Mob. One of them is Bratva—looks like he's been through the mill. As for the rest of the Russians, we've been able to get solid IDs off their fingerprints and security footage—a good thing because there wasn't much left of some of them.

"These guys have all got records a mile long, but adding kidnapping and extortion would help put them back behind bars," Hendricks continued. "Any of them look familiar?"

"The Russians shot all of the Newark goons at the rental house and took me to the warehouse," Ben said. "Then, between the second team of Newark guys and the ghosts, the rest of the Bratva team died. I recognize the Russian who's left, but I didn't get a good look at the last group of Newark goons."

"Both Newark and Bratva called me to trade Ben for the windows," Erik said for the record. "I was busy helping Ben escape during the shootout, and there were a lot of...distractions...so I didn't get a good look at either the Russians or the Jersey guys."

The Bratva mobster lunged for the cell door and shouted something in Russian. Erik snapped back in the same language, which left the man seething.

"You speak Russian?" Hendricks asked once they were out of the holding area.

"Only the swear words," Erik replied. "He called me an asshole, so I said his mother fucked donkeys."

Ben snickered. Hendricks shut his eyes and took a deep breath. "So much for a moment of international communication."

"My grasp of Italian is likewise limited to ordering off a menu and swearing like a sailor," Ben supplied. "Comes in handy."

They left the cell block, and Erik turned to Hendricks. "Do you really need us to ID anyone at the morgue if you've gotten fingerprints?" He could see how strained Ben looked and knew that while his partner was putting up a good front, the ordeal had taken a toll.

"I've got mug shots for the names we matched and some photos in the conference room, so we don't actually have to drive over," Hendricks said. "From where we found the bodies, there's no question about their involvement in this situation, but you might be able to add to what we know."

"Thank you," Erik said, and Ben agreed. Hendricks took them to where the morgue photos were laid out on a long table, a grim but familiar part of police work.

"I recognize all but three of them," Ben said. "Some were better about masking than others."

"I didn't get much of a look in the warehouse before all hell broke loose," Erik replied. "Then again, Mob foot soldiers are interchangeable and replaceable."

Hendricks had them both sign statements about the kidnapping, then walked them to the door. "I still don't claim to understand how you pulled that off, but thank you. It was a stinking mess to clean up, but the police body count would have been a lot higher without your woo-woo." He cleared his throat. "Unofficially."

"Thank you. Unofficially," Erik replied with a hint of a smile.

"Give my mom a call when you get a chance," Hendricks said. "I'm pretty sure that she's got casseroles and desserts to bring over."

"I will never turn down recuperation food," Ben told him. "And Susan is an amazing cook."

Hendricks rubbed his belly. "That's why I never miss Sunday dinner." He made a shooing motion. "Get going and try not to cause any new international incidents for a couple of weeks so I can catch up on the paperwork."

EIGHT

ERIK

E rik breathed a sigh of relief when they left police headquarters and saw Ben relax as well.

"Now what?" Ben asked.

"I'd like to take a drive past Weston Hall and a couple of other abandoned properties to throw anyone watching us off the scent," Erik replied. "I leveraged as much online information as I could, including drone footage and floor plans. But most of it wasn't recent. I'd like to get a look in daylight at what we're walking into after dark."

"Because you don't feel safe with just a witch, necromancer, and vampire?" Ben snickered.

"It would help to know whether they can drive a truck close enough to get the crates into it, if we find them," Erik replied. "Not to mention fences and gates. I'm not planning to get out of the car."

"It's the inside that worries me, if the place has been left to rot. Is Weston Hall truly abandoned, or just unused?" Ben asked.

"From everything I found, it's not being actively maintained," Erik said. "I gather that Bartolo's murder left his affairs in disarray, and there were legal battles that might still be going on. With no clear owner, a murky title, and no money or proxy dedicated to oversight, it's been truly abandoned."

"If they ever clear up the ownership, they'll have to tear it down," Ben observed. "There won't be anything worth salvaging."

"Except the stained glass," Erik said wistfully.

"Wait, it's got a dome too?"

"Different shape than the one from the Commodore Wilson. That was round. The one from Weston Hall arched over a hallway, long and narrow. It was pretty, but it wasn't said to be by Tiffany. It's a shame that it's been left there, but it's not our property or our problem," Erik said.

The sunny day was perfect for a drive. They opened the windows and turned up the radio, enjoying the road trip.

Cape May's tourism had been good to the hotels and restaurants in the area. Although there had been ups and downs, the number of historic and Victorian homes and hotels that survived were part of the town's appeal. When a big hotel struggled, it was usually bought by investors and renovated.

During some of the lean times in the town's economy, there had been a couple of notable exceptions that didn't find an angel investor. Weston Hall was one of those, deemed too old, needing too much remodeling to be profitable.

Erik headed first to the Sea Queen Hotel, which started as a private mansion and was turned into a bed and breakfast before falling on hard times. Tucked down a quiet street without an ocean view and not especially close to modern restaurants and attractions, investors hadn't been in a hurry to tear it down, even for the land. Now the once-opulent Victorian building sat behind a chain-link fence, paint peeling, roof sagging, and yard overgrown.

"It's always sad to see places like that," Ben said as they drove past the Sea Queen. "It was someone's dream, and lots of things can go wrong that aren't the owner's fault."

"The hospitality industry is notoriously fickle," Erik replied. "We hear about the people who make it big and create an empire, but lots of people lose their shirts."

Next came Weston Hall, a sprawling Second Empire building that rivaled the Inn at Cape May's architecture, even in decline. Erik could imagine how it must have looked before it fell on hard times.

"Probably safer going into the storage building than the attic," Ben observed. The property wasn't fenced, although weeds choked the land around it. "I see a back driveway for deliveries. Let's hope it has a way in that doesn't require stairs."

"If the Tiffany dome is there, someone got it inside in the first place, so there has to be a way to get it out." Erik didn't want to linger too long in case they were being watched, but he also wanted to get any details clear in his mind that the drone footage hadn't confirmed. "If all else fails, I'll get Haley to ask the ghosts."

The last property, another red herring, the McGill House, had once been the home of a wealthy sea captain and ended up as a restaurant that fell on hard times.

"I'm amazed that these were originally private homes," Ben said. "It's just sad that they didn't get taken care of properly."

They did their best to get a feel for how vulnerable they might be going back to Weston Hall that night. Erik checked his rearview mirror over and over throughout their drive, worried that not all of the mobsters who had been sent after them were dealt with. When they drove away from the McGill house, he spotted the same sedan that he had seen after the prior house and knew it couldn't be a coincidence. Unfortunately, he also knew it wasn't the undercover cop who'd been shadowing them.

"Shit. We've picked up a tail," Erik said. "Buckle up and hold on."

Erik knew his way around Cape May's streets, unlike their pursuers. The narrow thoroughfares in the older residential sections were often one lane and one-way. Traffic was light this time of day, which meant less chance of involving an innocent bystander in the encounter.

He wound around, doubling back more than once in an attempt to shake their pursuer. Since the Mob knew where to find their shop, he guessed that the car following them meant to hurt or kill them to throw them off the case.

The mobsters behind them could ram their car, shoot them, or blow out the tires, all of which could be fatal.

"Fuck that," he muttered. He glanced at Ben. "I've got an idea. Sit tight."

Erik remembered a speed trap where the Cape May cops often lay in wait to discourage fast driving in the old neighborhoods. He mentally crossed his fingers and hoped they were lying in wait as he sped up and watched the car behind them keep pace.

"Yes!" he said under his breath as he saw the squad car tucked into a hidden driveway. Erik revved the motor, floored the pedal, and laid on the horn as they zoomed past.

Before sirens had a chance to blare, the mobsters fired twice. Erik had been doing his best to weave back and forth from curb to curb, hoping to be difficult to hit. The shots missed, but Erik didn't trust that luck to hold forever.

If their speed and the horn didn't wake up the cop in his hideout, the gunfire certainly did. The squad car burned rubber pulling out of its hiding place, turned on the siren, and closed in on the mobsters' vehicle.

Erik cut the wheel hard to the right, sending them up on the curb but getting out from in front of the mobsters. Both the other vehicles sped by in a blur, and Erik hoped that no one got hurt. He knew the cop's camera had recorded his license plate and expected a call from the chief. Though at this point he wouldn't be surprised if all the cops in Cape May knew his Highlander and Ben's Mustang on sight.

"You, okay?" Ben asked, and Erik realized how hard his heart was pounding. "Nice driving."

"Yeah, I'm all right. You?"

Ben nodded. "I might have a bruise from the seatbelt on my shoulder, but that beats hell out of a gunshot wound."

Erik and Ben kept a close eye on the rearview mirrors for the rest of the drive, but no other pursuers surfaced. Erik drove around the block three times when they got to the shop and apartment, making sure none of the parked cars were occupied or suspicious.

If they really want us gone, they'll try to blow up the building. We're warded up the wazoo, so it won't work, but they can try.

He realized that Ben had drawn his gun, keeping it in hand but out of sight as Erik parked the SUV and they hurried to the door. No one approached them, and no shots rang out, although the mobsters certainly had the address.

Once they were inside and away from the windows, both men breathed a sigh of relief.

"Wasn't really expecting needing to out-drive an assassin," Erik said once they were inside the apartment with the door locked. His voice and his hands shook, but he figured he had earned it.

"Nice driving." Ben sounded equally shaken. "My super-spy saves the day."

Erik acknowledged the endearment with a rueful smile. "I'm just trying to figure out what the hell that was all about. I get following us. They figure we know where the window is, and they want us to lead them to it. But shooting us is messy. It draws attention from the authorities and complicates their getting to the prize."

"Want to bet that was an overachieving underling wanting to score points?" Ben replied. "In my experience, the foot soldiers weren't always the brightest."

Erik made them both hot tea and sat in the kitchen for a while to lose the jitters. His phone rang half an hour after they got back.

"Mitchell, Nolan, what the hell just happened?" Chief Hendricks barked.

"We went out for a drive, and someone followed us and tried to shoot us," Erik replied, pleased he managed to sound calm, even blasé.

"I got that much. Who and why?" the chief snapped.

"We're guessing one of the bosses put a tail on us to lead them to the missing dome from the Commodore Wilson," Erik said. "And when we didn't, they improvised and shot at us."

"Jesus. Do you *know* where the dome is?" the chief returned.

"No," Erik replied, which was technically the truth, despite their suspicions. "And if we did, we'd tell you." *After our team removed it to a supernatural supermax.*

Hendricks made a skeptical noise but didn't argue. "I want to be kept in the loop, Mitchell. You hear me?"

Erik appreciated Hendricks's tenacity, but he also knew that while the cops might be able to go up against regular gangsters, the supernatural aspect of this case was out of their league. There would be plenty of time for the cops to help with the cleanup that was less likely to get anyone hexed.

"We hear you," Ben replied, making sure the chief knew he had them both paying attention. "And we appreciated the squad car coming to the rescue. Did they catch the shooters?"

Hendricks swore under his breath. "No. The mobsters caused a traffic accident and got away. I'm sure the car was stolen, so getting the license number isn't likely to lead anywhere. We'll probably find the car abandoned and wiped clean."

"You never know," Erik said. "Sometimes they get sloppy. You could get a break."

"Keep your heads down and your hands clean," Hendricks told them, ignoring Erik's last comment. "And try not to get killed. My mother would be very upset." He ended the call before Erik had a chance to reply.

"Considering everything, Hendricks took that pretty well, I think," Erik said.

Ben chuckled. "About as well as possible. I know the police academy doesn't prepare you for guys like us, or at least it wasn't covered in *my* training. I'm sure he's also pissed that he thought it was safe to take the plainclothesman off our tail. Don't be surprised if our shadow returns."

Once they got settled, Ben put his detective skills to work to see if he could find drone footage or urban-explorer videos of Weston Hall that Erik hadn't already viewed.

Erik called Alessia. "Are you and Haley together? I have another favor to ask. Would you be up for a quick video call?"

"We're just stress eating and drinking some emotional support wine," Alessia said, and Erik heard Haley's laughter in the background. "Sure. I'll open up the meeting space."

Erik and Ben stuck with coffee for now, although Erik planned on adding something stronger once he was sure they were settled for the evening. He opened his laptop and started the video meeting. Alessia and Haley waved.

"What do you need?" Haley asked.

"I think I know where the missing Tiffany dome from the Commodore Wilson might be," Erik replied. "We've done research and checked drone footage, but I'd like to know for sure before we go tramping around a deserted old hotel. I wondered if the ghosts could answer a few questions."

"Sure, we can try," Haley said, and Alessia nodded.

Erik gave them a quick recap about the dome and why they zeroed in on Weston Hall as Haley rustled through her bag and set up for a reading.

"Please tell me you aren't going in by yourself," Alessia said. "Much as I loathe cobwebs, if you need me, I can be backup."

"Ditto," Haley offered as she lit a bundle of sage and a candle and set down a salt circle around the table.

"Thank you," Ben said. "We contacted the people who can take both the dome and the haunted window out of here and hide them forever. I'm hoping that having a witch, a necromancer, and a vampire with us will be enough."

Alessia laughed. "Bringing out the big guns? I like that plan."

Haley finished her preparations and took a few deep breaths to relax while Alessia activated wards for protection. Summoning spirits carried risk, since there was no guarantee who might actually show up.

"Spirits of Weston Hall. I need to ask questions. Please come to me," Haley said, eyes still closed.

"What do you want to know?" Haley channeled the spirit's question in a voice not quite her own.

Erik already knew that Cape May homes built when Weston Hall was constructed rarely had basements because of the high water table. Instead, some had a non-public space beneath the main floor that served for above-ground storage. That elevated the porch and living areas, further protecting them from flooding, and also created a place for the mechanical systems and items that usually went in a cellar.

But given how large the dome was and how many crates it would take up, he strongly doubted it was stored in the hotel itself, which made Erik zero in on the former conference center's warehouse as the most likely storage site.

"Can you go into the storage building and tell me what you see? I'm looking for several large wooden crates with shipping labels on them," Erik told the ghost. "If anything is blocking the entrance, tell me. Afterward, our friends can help you pass over if you want."

Haley nodded somberly. "It would be good to move on. I will try."

Haley remained still as Erik guessed the ghost left to check the warehouse. They waited for a few minutes, hoping he would return.

"There are a lot of boxes and crates. But eight are long and very tall. They don't appear to have been opened," Haley reported.

Erik knew from his research that the dome at the Commodore Wilson had a 27-foot diameter and eight individual panels, like the slices of a pie.

"That's it," Erik said, excited that his hunch had paid off. "Anything dangerous like a collapsed ceiling?"

Ghosts could come and go despite the condition of the warehouse, but Erik and his friends had vulnerable human bodies.

"It does not look like anyone has been inside for a long time. Nothing has collapsed, but I cannot speak to safety," Haley answered.

"How about a way in and out?" Ben added.

"There are large overhead doors on one end in addition to a couple of standard doors. The driveway is covered with debris." Haley's voice took on a dreamy quality that wasn't part of her normal tone. She opened her eyes and gave a full-body shudder as the ghost left her.

"Thank you," Haley said to the spirit, fully herself again. "Would you like to pass over now?" she asked the ghost.

Ben and Erik couldn't see what actually happened, but Erik envisioned a doorway of light. In his mind's eye, he saw the spirit walk through the opening and vanish as the glow dimmed.

"Did you get what you needed?" Alessia asked as Haley drank a glass of water and nibbled a cookie to replenish after channeling the ghost.

"Yes. The good news is that those crates sound exactly like what I'd expect for the dome, and it doesn't seem like anyone has bothered them in thirty years," Erik replied.

"And the bad news?" Ben prompted.

"There are a lot of them, and they're going to be awkward and heavy as well. It's going to take a full-sized semi-trailer truck. Since no one has tended the property in a long time, the driveway to the storage area has storm debris," Erik said.

"At least you know for certain that they're where you thought," Alessia said.

"Thank you both so much for everything," Erik replied. "We'll let you know how it goes." With that, he ended the video call, promising to get together soon for lunch, without mobsters or the impending end of the world.

"I'm guessing that Rowan and Donnelly could use magic to clear the driveway," Ben said. "As for the containers, let them know about the dimensions and weight, and they'll figure it out."

Erik sent a text to Cassidy, knowing she would let the rest of the team know. He looked up at Ben. "How about you? Find more footage?"

Ben brought his laptop over and sat down next to Erik. He had several windows open and pulled up the first one.

"Here's a flyover from four months ago," Ben said. "Other than the storm that just finished, there haven't been a lot of high winds to bring down branches or trees. You can make out the service drive here." He pointed with a pencil. "It doesn't look like there are large pieces blocking it."

He switched windows on his screen. "Here's a video from some explorers who got inside the main hotel." The clip was only about ten minutes long, and the dark surroundings made it difficult to pick up details.

"Ignore the chatter," Ben instructed. "The important thing is that they didn't seem to be dodging holes in the floor or fallen ceilings. That bodes well if we need to go inside, though I'm thinking we may just need to enter the storage building."

A couple more exploration videos revealed a remarkably well-preserved interior, despite mold and cobwebs. Shaky cameras and breathless voice-overs were part of the deal for the amateur explorers or paranormal investigators.

"Any self-respecting ghost would have stayed hidden," Erik observed.

"Look here." Ben pointed. "I think this is the stained-glass corridor dome you mentioned."

The videos were shot at night, so no daylight streamed in through the glass. Instead, someone shone a bright spotlight onto the narrow dome while the camera zoomed in.

"It's actually in pretty good shape, considering," Erik remarked. "I hope that the video doesn't give looters or vandals any ideas."

"I was thinking the same thing," Ben agreed. "But the original stained-glass archway backs up your theory on why the old owner wanted to add the dome from the Commodore Wilson."

"Too bad he couldn't pull it off," Erik said. "It would have been spectacular."

They made sandwiches and ate a quick lunch, then opted for some sleep since it would be a late night. They were both keyed up about the evening's work, so they were content to kiss and cuddle but not take it further.

Erik slept hard enough that he felt disoriented when he woke a few hours later. They still had time before they were due to meet Sorren and the others, so Erik went to make an early dinner while Ben checked email.

His phone buzzed, and a message from Sorren gave an estimated arrival time, as well as confirmation of the meeting point behind Weston Hall. A picture of a semi-truck made Erik feel better about the logistics, and he hoped the vehicle came with a forklift and crew. They'd managed to get the dome into the warehouse, so it had to be possible to move it out.

"I know this qualifies as an adventure," Ben said as they got dressed for the night's work. "But I'm officially ready for some time off when no one is trying to kill us."

"Right there with you," Erik agreed. "Don't forget, we still have to get through the autumn festival."

Ben groaned. "Signing up to volunteer seemed like a good idea at the time."

Erik chuckled. "Susan really didn't leave us a lot of choice about playing a role. It was just about which role we wanted to play."

Susan took her community responsibilities seriously, something that Erik usually found endearing. She was a committed booster for anything that helped showcase Cape May or contributed to a better quality of living.

Since the Awesome Autumn Festival raised money for the local library, museums, preservation work, and other causes, Erik didn't begrudge being drafted into service and knew that under normal circumstances, Ben didn't mind, either. Before they left for their rendezvous with Sorren and the others, Erik got the haunted stained-glass panel out of the safe and put it in the back of the SUV. He left it in the spell-dampening box with the protective blanket, but still felt uncomfortable.

"I'll be glad to be rid of that thing," Ben said, putting Erik's thoughts into words. "I know it was all locked up with magic, but I felt like it was still watching us."

Erik had wrestled with that same feeling despite knowing the wards on the safe were strong. He was just as happy to hand it off to Sorren along with the Tiffany dome.

———

Although they had just driven to Weston Hall earlier in the day, by night the road looked very different. Erik was grateful that the area around the abandoned hotel was sparsely developed, since hiding a truck large enough to remove the crates of window panels would be difficult even with magic.

A security light by the road did not reach all the way to the back of Weston Hall or the warehouse. None of the hotel's lights were lit. Erik suspected that their friends might not need the illumination, but he and Ben definitely did, and they both wore night-vision goggles.

To his relief, the truck was already in place when they arrived. While it certainly wasn't invisible, Erik realized that his gaze just seemed to slide away, and the vehicle didn't stick in his memory, something he attributed to Rowan's magic.

"Erik, Ben, happy to see you both in good health," Sorren greeted them. "I'm sure you remember Rowan and Donnelly."

Erik and Ben nodded, knowing that many people with magic preferred not to shake hands.

"We got ghostly confirmation that what we want is inside, but it's going to be heavy and hard to move," Erik told them. "And Ben and I will need light to keep from falling over ourselves."

"We've got you covered." Rowan murmured a spell, opening one of the big overhead doors and casting a glow inside. The truck had been backed up to the dock, ready to load.

"We brought a very trustworthy crew to load the crates," she told them. "The truck and the crew are protected by magic."

"Donnelly and I will go in first, with Erik and Ben behind us, and Rowan covering our backs," Sorren said. "We're harder to kill."

Since Sorren was already technically undead, Erik guessed that was vampire humor.

The warehouse held a hodgepodge of equipment. Mildewed cardboard boxes stacked against the back wall had disintegrated, spilling their contents onto the bare floor. Rusted folding chairs and banquet tables were piled in another area. From what Erik could make out, the long-forgotten items were what he would expect from a hotel and conference center, with the exception of the crates from the auction.

The witch light illuminated the area well enough to see where they were going but was unlikely to attract attention outside. The crates from the Commodore Wilson were clustered near the door, delivered and forgotten. They were all large and looked heavy. Erik tried to remember what other architectural pieces Bartolo had bought from the liquidation sale.

"Over there." Erik pointed toward the tall, long boxes.

Donnelly approached the crates with caution, and Erik guessed that the necromancer was scanning for hostile magic.

"There's definitely *something* going on with the dome." Donnelly paused for a moment. "A redirection spell and perhaps something hiding it. Rowan, if you wouldn't mind?"

They waited while Rowan looked over the crates and chanted a spell that Erik couldn't quite catch. "Done. It was already weakening, but you should be able to sense it now. Though that means anyone else looking for it can as well. The sooner we get it within the wards on the truck, the better." Rowan stepped back, and Donnelly resumed his inspection.

"I suspect the dome's magic has been weakened by so long without light or people around, so it may be dormant, for now. The photos were beautiful, but there's a darkness about the pieces." Donnelly frowned. "Subtle, but definitely real. If it's still discernible after all this time, I'd hate to think what it was like installed where it got sunlight and exposure to people. It definitely needs to go somewhere that can keep it, and everyone else, safe."

"I have the haunted window in a box in our SUV," Erik reminded them. "I'll hand it off when we're ready to go."

Donnelly's head came up as if alerted to something only he could hear. Erik sensed that the ghosts of Weston Hall had taken notice of them.

"We mean you no harm," Donnelly spoke into the darkness. "I'm sure having this stored here over the years was uncomfortable. We'll take it away, and I'll be glad to send anyone on who wants to go."

Erik hadn't thought about how the dome's negative vibes might have affected the old hotel's resident ghosts, but he could imagine it as a constant irritant. They were lucky it hadn't turned the spirits angry and dangerous.

"How are we doing out there, Rowan?" Sorren looked toward the entranceway where Rowan had returned.

"Nothing so far," she replied. "Let's get this show on the road."

Black-clad workers swarmed from the truck, maneuvering a forklift. Ben and Erik stood back and let Sorren and Donnelly direct the crew, who didn't seem to find the circumstances strange in the least.

Rowan remained on alert from attackers outside. After Donnelly's comment to the ghosts clarifying that they weren't thieves, Erik wasn't worried about the spirits turning on them. Ben and Erik carried their guns in case mobsters showed up.

As the crates left the warehouse and the truck was loaded, Erik wondered if it was his imagination that the vibe shifted. He hadn't been aware of a heaviness when they first arrived, but the more pieces of the dome that left the area, the more the energy cleared.

"I wonder if buying the dome is what got Bartolo killed?" Ben mused aloud. "And if it contributed to the hotel's downfall."

"I wouldn't doubt it," Rowan replied as Donnelly and Sorren directed placement of the last crates onto the truck. "Makes me wonder about the origin of the dome. Some pieces are just born bad, but that's usually by design. If the dome was commissioned for its original site, the artist had it in for them."

Erik thought of the Commodore Wilson's checkered past, unlucky even before the bombastic preacher took over. None of the prior owners had lasted long, and most either died young or were financially ruined by the huge old hotel. Against that history, the dome seemed like a poisonous flower, beautiful but deadly.

Donnelly stood in the center of the warehouse and turned in a slow circle, one hand outstretched. "I did a sweep of the building to make sure we got all the pieces. Definitely don't want to leave any of that bad mojo behind." He turned to Sorren, who was standing with the crew chief.

"We've got them all. Go ahead and lock it up," he said as the last of the workers climbed back inside and the driver took his seat in the cab. The semi rumbled to life and pulled cautiously out of the darkened driveway.

Rowan secured the door to the warehouse and dimmed the

conjured light to a glow of fire above her palm so they could see each other as they talked.

"Here's the haunted window," Erik returned with the spelled case, taking it to Soren's SUV. "Good riddance. I hope you've got plenty of magic on this car and that semi."

"Layers upon layers," Donnelly assured them. "One of the crew is a talented witch. They'll be okay—and so will we. The dome is now hidden again from anyone trying to scry for it."

"Thank you for taking the windows off our hands," Ben said. "There's no real owner, and it was going to be a reason for The Collector and The Oligarch to keep poking around until someone found it."

"The Alliance is aware of both men," Sorren said with a definite tone of distaste. "We do our best to keep the worst items, like the dome, out of their hands. The underground trade in cursed and haunted objects is regrettably brisk."

Given the death and damage Erik had witnessed with non-magical artwork in his years with Interpol, he didn't envy the Alliance their task.

Donnelly walked back over to Erik and Ben. "Good to see you. Nice work on this. Try to stay out of trouble for a while." He winked and got into the passenger seat.

"From him, that's high praise," Rowan confided before she joined Donnelly. "But you two had the odds stacked against you and still came out on top. That's something to be proud of. Take care."

That left Sorren, the last to leave. "Nice work. Thank you for keeping Cassidy in the loop. I know Charleston isn't close, but when it's important, we can get here. Call us when you need us." Sorren slid behind the wheel and turned on the engine.

Erik and Ben got into their Highlander and led the way, with Sorren's SUV behind them. They didn't turn their lights on until they were on the main road.

Erik's phone rang with a call from Rowan, and he put it on speaker. "Heads up," she warned. "The ghosts say there's a roadblock just down the road. Six black SUVs and at least a dozen men with weapons. I'm sensing someone with strong magic too."

"Sounds like a mobster welcoming committee," Ben muttered. "If The Collector or The Oligarch has been tailing us, maybe one of them decided to come in person to get the dome. Did the semi get through?"

"Yes," Rowan replied. "We sent them in the opposite direction to take a roundabout route just in case something like this happened. They have magic and protections, but I'm hoping that they won't need them. In that way, us drawing unwanted attention gives the truck a better chance to escape."

"We're right behind you," Rowan continued. "Donnelly's stirred up the ghosts to cause trouble, but we're not likely to get past the goons without a fight."

"We're armed," Erik replied. "Handguns, not machine guns."

"I'll disable their firearms," Rowan said confidently. "And handle the magic of The Collector or Oligarch, if they're here. Sorren will help take out the trash. We've got this."

Something deep in the pit of Erik's gut told him they had overlooked something, but he just nodded. "Roger that. Be careful."

They spotted a firing squad of men in black fatigues, leveling machine guns at them.

"Hope Rowan is right about the guns, or this isn't going to go well," Erik muttered. Just in case, he turned to Ben. "I love you."

"Love you too. And I'm betting on our side," Ben reached over and squeezed Erik's arm.

A tall man in a dark jacket stepped forward, confirming Erik's worst fears.

"That's him—The Collector. Remo Barone," Erik said under his breath. "Damn. He came in person."

"He's a witch?" Ben's voice betrayed his tension.

"Yeah. Pretty powerful, by all accounts," Erik answered.

"Give us the dome!" Barone yelled.

Sorren's vehicle was parked behind their SUV, with the lights on and the engine still running. A glance in the rearview mirror told Erik that Rowan and the others were no longer inside, although he hadn't seen them leave.

"Don't shoot," Erik called back after rolling down the window. "We don't have the dome. It's still in the warehouse." He and Ben stayed in their SUV, hoping Rowan's magical protections held.

The night had grown unseasonably cold, and frost began to form on the windshield. *Donnelly's ghosts, waiting to make an entrance*, Erik thought as he sensed spirits massing around them. The roar of several large SUVs behind the Newark mobsters halted the conversation. Metal crunched, and men shouted and swore as the new SUVs rammed into the mobsters' vehicles and guns fired.

Erik and Ben ducked but stayed in their warded vehicle, counting on their friends to handle the new attack. They peered over the dashboard, needing to know what was happening.

More men with guns were silhouetted in the headlights, along with a tall man in a long coat that Erik knew had to be Konstantin Gusev, The Oligarch.

"Put down your weapons," Gusev ordered in a thick Russian accent. "We will take the dome."

"Like hell," Barone muttered, and a twitch of his fingers had the Newark mobsters pivoting to open fire on the Russians, except that nothing happened.

"Fire!" Gusev ordered, and while his soldiers took aim, the guns jammed.

That's got to be Rowan's magic, Erik thought, heart thudding since he had been sure they were about to be mowed down.

Everything happened at once. Mobsters from both factions rushed each other, only to be thrown back by magical protections. They turned on Sorren's SUV and Erik's vehicle but didn't get within five feet before an invisible force tossed them through the air. A gray whirlwind of angry spirits rushed toward both sets of mobsters. The ghosts wailed and screeched, showing themselves as spectral corpses with open maws and skeletal, grasping hands, making themselves heard to everyone.

The SUVs' headlights blinked out, leaving them in darkness.

A foxfire-green glow radiated from the ghosts, like in a horror movie. Terrified foot soldiers tried to fire at the apparitions, then dropped their useless guns and fled into the woods. A tide of green and white spirits followed, and from deep within the marshy woodlands, Erik heard screams of terror, men begging for their lives in English and Russian, and moments later, it went suddenly silent.

"Holy shit," Ben muttered.

Neither weapons nor fighting prowess helped the gangsters against angry ghosts. Ben and Erik watched the revenants close in on the toughs who stayed on the road. Some men fell down dead without a sound. Others struggled and screamed against an unseen force that lifted them from the ground before flinging their broken bodies toward the trees.

Erik suspected that the ghosts who could make themselves visible spent their energy terrorizing their victims. Now and then, among the gray shapes, he spotted darker shadows of unnatural creatures snatching men and carrying them away. Stories said this stretch of road and the wetlands around it were haunted, maybe even cursed. Creatures that hungered for flesh and blood were said to dwell in the marshes. If so, Erik wondered if they got their fill.

When the headlights came back on, Rowan held a fist out in front of her, magically immobilizing both The Collector and The Oligarch. Their guns lay in a pile next to where Sorren stood. The look of concentration on Donnelly's face told Erik that the necromancer had awakened the marsh spirits and kept enough control to protect the group on the road.

"Release us immediately!" Barone sputtered in fury. Gusev shouted something in Russian, and Erik remembered enough to know it was a similar command. Rowan twitched her fingers, and they fell silent, still red-faced from screaming with the cords on their necks standing out with strain.

"Remo Barone and Konstantin Gusev, you are hereby called to account to be soul-judged for your crimes, which are many." Donnelly turned to the two Mob bosses who struggled against their invisible bonds.

"I will read your souls, which cannot hide the truth," Donnelly continued. "You will witness your soul's testimony, and judgment will be passed. Behold."

Donnelly gestured toward the two prisoners, and their previous defiance vanished, replaced with silent screams of utter terror.

Erik figured being confronted with your greatest sins would be sobering under any circumstances. For Barone and Gusev, with countless murders and felonies to their account, any pretense of rationalization appeared to have been stripped away, leaving them to face the merciless judge of their own memories.

"You are found guilty of the crimes etched into your souls," Donnelly intoned. "You will be punished by the ghosts of your victims. Judgment is passed."

A red mist formed above Gusev and Barone, swirling like a whirlwind of blood. The temperature dropped again, sending fingers of frost across the windshields. Erik shivered, more from primal fear than from the cold. Faces appeared in the vortex, and then it dropped to enfold both crime bosses.

Rowan gestured, and the terrified death shrieks of the two mobsters rang in Erik's ears. His stomach turned at the smell of blood and entrails that reached them even inside the SUV. Streams of blood escaped the whirlwind to soak the road.

When the red storm dissipated, all that remained were two piles of broken bones, tattered clothing scraps, and shredded bits of skin and muscle, hardly enough to have been two grown men.

Erik hadn't seen Sorren move until the vampire emerged from the woods next to the road. "The swamp took the ones who ran," he said. "There are no survivors."

Rowan looked at Erik and Ben, who hadn't moved from the SUV, still trying to process the horror of what they had just witnessed. "We need to go."

Erik thought he felt a nudge of compulsion in her voice, enough to break through the mental fog.

"We'll lead the way. Follow us," Rowan said. "There was a turn about a mile back that should take us to an alternate route. Go straight home. We'll head for Charleston." Rowan watched them intently as if to ensure they were listening.

Erik glanced at the cars and guns, avoiding another look at what remained of Barone and Gusev.

"Leave them. There is nothing to implicate you. Let them be a warning," Rowan answered his unvoiced question. "We need to go. The magic and blood have awakened more than ghosts. We shouldn't linger."

Erik didn't want to know what entities were fearsome enough to make their protectors flee the scene. He didn't need to be convinced to leave, and from the shellshocked look on Ben's face, Erik knew his partner agreed. Rowan's magic cleared away the roadblock and the other vehicles enough for them to pass.

Released from the magic, the Highlander shifted into gear without issue. Erik followed the SUV with Sorren and the others until they reached the ramp to the highway. Erik turned back toward Cape May, while the others turned south. He assumed the truck was already well on its way.

"Are you okay?" Erik ventured when they had ridden in silence for several minutes.

"Hell no. You?" Ben replied.

"Trying to figure out if we have enough whiskey at home to ever let me sleep again," Erik admitted.

"Not sure there's enough whiskey in the world for that," Ben replied.

Erik reached over and took Ben's hand. "We're alive. Barone, Gusev, and their goons will never hurt anyone again. The dome and the window will be locked away where they can't cause more harm. We're safe."

"I knew Rowan and the others were powerful," Ben said. "But I didn't realize—"

"Neither did I. For a couple of minutes there, when I wasn't sure we were going to die, I felt like I'd been dropped into an action movie," Erik admitted.

"Except not the fun kind of movie," Ben replied. "The kind that gives you PTSD with a side order of night terrors."

"Yeah." Erik paused. "You know we need to call Hendricks."

"I figured you were going to say that," Ben replied. "And I wish I could argue, but I can't."

The clock said midnight, but Erik felt like it was much later.

"I want to report a multi-vehicle accident," Erik said when the dispatcher answered. He gave the road and approximate location. "Cars blocking the road, but no one in sight."

He hung up without giving his name, but he knew his number would show up in the system and that Hendricks would call in the morning.

They rode in silence for a while. Erik figured it was a combination of exhaustion and decompression after all the recent danger and tension. When no one appeared to be following them, he breathed a sigh of relief. "So…after all that, what's on your mind?"

"Ask me in the morning. Right now, I can barely remember my name," Ben admitted.

NINE

BEN

Early the next morning, Hendricks showed up at their door. "You've got some serious explaining to do." He barely waited for Erik to invite him in.

"We called you," Erik replied. "Gave you a heads up."

Hendricks looked at them incredulously. "You called the station, and nothing about that scene was a normal multi-vehicle accident except that it looked like several of the vehicles had rammed into each other. The cars track back to the Newark Mob and Bratva. The weapons are unregistered, highly illegal, and still loaded with ammunition. A dozen corpses were floating in the marsh, and piles of bloody goop and bones were in the road, as well as a bunch of dead goons—some without a mark on them. Forensics is working on the teeth and DNA to get solid IDs. How in the hell—"

"We called in reinforcements with special abilities to help us safely move the dome to where it couldn't hurt anyone else," Erik said.

"What do you mean by 'special abilities'?" Hendricks demanded.

Ben took it as a good sign that Hendricks had come to them instead of having them brought down to the station. He figured that the chief suspected supernatural elements were involved.

"A witch, a necromancer, and a vampire," Erik replied as if there was nothing special about the admission. He thought it best to leave Haley and Alessia out of his explanation.

"Don't joke around."

"We're not," Ben replied. "You asked. That's the truth. We got ambushed by Barone's people, and then Gusav's goons ambushed *them*. Magic jammed the guns, or there would have been an epic shootout. Then the ghosts chased the foot soldiers into the marsh and took their vengeance on Barone and Gusev. I apologize for not calling you directly. We were rattled and maybe not thinking clearly by then."

"Why aren't you dead?" Hendricks looked like he was struggling to put the pieces together.

"The witch protected us," Erik said. "Fortunately, her magic was stronger than theirs."

"I can't put that into a report."

"Blame a creature of unknown origin," Ben suggested. "Say it made hash of Barone and Gusev and some of their henchmen, and the rest of the terrified goons ran into the marsh and drowned."

"You want me to falsify information."

Erik met his gaze. "As far as you're concerned, witches, necromancers, and vampires *are* 'creatures of unknown origin.' Or you can tell the whole truth, but I doubt it will go well."

Hendricks ran a hand over his eyes. His pained expression suggested a migraine. "Do your friends pose a danger to the community?"

"No. They're the good guys. And they're already gone, along with the dome."

Ben didn't want to admit to trespassing at Weston Hall, but since the property's ownership was in limbo, he doubted there was anyone to press charges.

"I'm guessing they took that small window too?" the chief asked.

"It won't cause any more trouble, ever again," Erik assured him.

Hendricks had the look of a man who had just discovered that a whole different reality lay hidden behind how he had always understood the world to work. "These people you called in—you already knew them. You've worked with them before."

"They're allies and friends," Ben replied. "Working quietly in the shadows to keep the world safe so most people can go about their business and never even suspect the supernatural is real."

"Trinkets has been in Cape May for a long time," Hendricks said. "Has it always done this kind of thing?"

Erik nodded. "Yes. It's one of many shops across the world that get dangerous magical items out of the wrong hands. That part is a mission, not a business."

"How much does Susan know? Is she safe working here?" Hendricks looked lost.

"She knows that magic is real and that there are bad guys out there with paranormal abilities," Erik replied. "We've given her protective charms and warded her house. I can't be sure what she suspects, but we don't involve her in the details."

"My first inclination is to make sure she stays far away from you two, to keep her safe," Hendricks admitted. "But if your people took out two Mafia hit teams, then maybe she's safest close to you."

"I think that's up to Susan," Ben reminded him. "She's pretty formidable all on her own."

Hendricks nodded. "I know. Doesn't change me wanting to protect her. Please, promise me you'll watch out for her."

"Absolutely," Ben swore.

Hendricks let out a long breath. "What you've told me is absolutely bonkers...and the only explanation that really fits the situation. God help me, it's going to take some creative writing on that report."

"Look at the bright side," Erik replied. "Any town that can take out Gusev and Bartolo without a small war is going to get noticed by both the Mob and Bratva. My bet is that both sides will steer clear of Cape May for quite a while."

"Probably too much to hope for, but I hope you're right." Hendricks looked from Erik to Ben. "I'm grateful that you didn't let the town get turned into a battleground, and I appreciate that you let me know about the wreck. But this does not mean that you are above the law. Do I make myself clear?"

"Absolutely," Erik said.

"Definitely," Ben echoed.

"I'll hold you to that. And I expect to stay in the loop," Hendricks said as he headed for the door.

They watched him get into his squad car and drive away.

"That went better than I thought it would," Erik observed. "Got any thoughts?"

Ben turned toward him. "I want to get a dog."

"A dog?" Erik said with a dumbfounded expression at the sudden shift in topic.

"Now seems like as good a time as we're ever going to get." Ben knew he sounded slightly defensive. "We've had one big threat after another, but with the windows taken care of and the mobsters set back on their heels—at least for now—we're reasonably safe. That might be a false sense of security; there are still other bad guys out there, but maybe we'll get lucky and have a break for a while."

"There's no way to know if things are really going to calm down," Erik warned.

"I know. But we can't put everything on hold forever until the world straightens itself out."

"You haven't mentioned it before, but I'm guessing this isn't a new thing," Erik said.

"I've been thinking about it for a while. I loved having dogs when I was growing up. My schedule was too crazy as a cop, and then my old boyfriend didn't like pets. But now, I don't have to work as long hours most of the time. Jenny would be fine with me bringing the dog to the office, I'm sure." Ben paused, feeling nervous. "Say something."

He hadn't brought up the subject before this. Their relationship had been too new, then there were several dangerous cases to contend with, and moving in together kept them busy. But now that they were settled into the apartment and their lives were as quiet as they were ever likely to get, Ben figured the timing could work.

"I guess a hellhound or shifter is out?" Erik's tone told Ben he was only partly joking.

"As much as that might come in handy from time to time, I mean a real, regular, non-magical canine," Ben clarified.

"I'm okay with that," Erik replied, and Ben felt himself relax. "Probably not a huge dog since we don't have much of a yard, but a small or medium-sized one would work." He paused. "Did you have a particular breed in mind?"

"I've always been partial to Golden Retrievers or Labradors," Ben admitted, knowing they didn't qualify as small or medium. "I fell in love with them from movies and TV shows. I know they're not small, but they're so friendly and smart…and easy to train. But if we get a rescue, I'm open to a Heinz 57," he added, meaning a mixed breed. "How about you?"

Erik had a faraway expression as he answered. "I didn't have a dog when I was a kid, but I always wanted one. When I got my own place, I worked long hours, and then when I started doing fraud and theft investigations with Interpol, I traveled too much. But if we can find the right dog, it would be nice."

"We'll need to make sure it doesn't freak out around magic," Ben said. "I've heard that dogs can pick up on the supernatural."

"I don't know about dogs, but cats can certainly sense ghosts," Erik said. "Magic is manipulated energy, and dogs have more acute senses than we do, so I guess it would make sense that they'd pick up on something."

"We don't have to get a puppy if you think that's too much work," Ben blurted. He had been thinking this through for a while and tried to counter all the obstacles. "We could get a young rescue dog. He'd be a little more settled. I'm not really stuck on a particular breed."

"You've really put thought into this." Erik's smile tugged at the corners of his mouth.

Ben sighed. "Guilty as charged. I didn't know when it might work, but I don't think our lives are ever going to slow down a whole lot more than what we've got. So now could be a good time."

"Okay."

Ben had his counterarguments all prepared, so Erik's agreement stopped him in his tracks. "Okay?"

Erik chuckled. "Yes. I'm fine with getting a dog, but it has to like both of us. My aunt and uncle had a chihuahua who loved her and pissed in my uncle's shoes."

"Got it. No shoe-peeing," Ben said. "I think we can work with that."

Erik looked thoughtful. "Getting a dog means needing dog things: bed, dish, water bowl, toys, other stuff. If we get the supplies before we get the dog, we don't know for sure what size we need. But if we wait to get the dog first, then we don't have the stuff when we all get home."

"I thought about that," Ben replied. "If we go to the big shelter, there are a couple of stores we could stop at on the way home. Take the dog with us and help pick stuff out."

"Okay, that could work, especially if it's already grown and not a little puppy," Erik agreed. "Boy or girl?"

"I've tried not to get my heart set on too many details up front," Ben admitted. "I was hoping it would be one of those 'love at first sight' things and we'd just know the right one."

Erik nodded. "I like that. Almost letting the dog pick us. When do you want to go? How about first thing in the morning?"

"Really?" Ben felt poleaxed, but his heart thudded in excitement. "Oh, my God."

Erik laughed. "Yes. Unless you've got something else going on. We don't have anything coming up for the next while, so we could be home to get everyone settled in. Before we have the next potentially world-ending supernatural catastrophe."

Ben stepped forward and kissed Erik on the lips. "I love you so much! Thank you from the bottom of my heart."

Erik kissed him back. "You know, we need to decide if the dog gets to sleep on the bed. I've heard that dogs can be almost as disruptive to sexy times as small children."

"Long-lasting chew toys. Bribery is a great distraction," Ben said. "I've gotten tips from other couples. We'll figure it out." Ben threw his arms around Erik. "We're getting a dog!"

Tired as they were, despite the late hour, Ben couldn't help looking around the apartment as they got ready for bed.

"We could put the dog bed there, or there." He pointed to the foot of their bed or a nearby corner. "Food dish and water bowl can go in the kitchen nook, where we won't trip over them. We'll find out what the shelter has been feeding it and pick up some of that food for starters."

"We can ask around for a good vet," Erik added as he stripped out of his clothes and pulled on sleep shorts and a T-shirt.

Ben watched him disrobe appreciatively, knowing that they were both too tired to do anything strenuous tonight. Even the buzz of excitement over becoming dog parents would fade, and they would crash and burn with exhaustion after all that had happened.

"We'll need a ball, toys, a collar and leash, plus a harness for in the car." Ben stripped and dressed for bed.

"Didn't know you were into that," Erik teased.

Ben rolled his eyes. "Stuff for a bath—for the dog. And we need to find out about dog training classes. It's a big commitment."

Erik pulled him close. "It is. And we're up to it. But I'm dead on my feet. So try to stop bouncing, and let's get some sleep so we can get to the morning faster."

Ben kissed him again. "I'm going to see if I can put myself to sleep thinking of dog names like counting sheep."

They climbed into bed and kissed again, slower this time but without heat or urgency. Just being warm and comfortable helped to slow Ben's racing thoughts, and he felt the exertion of the last few days begin to take its toll.

———

Ben woke in the morning, having slept like a rock. Nightmares didn't wake him, and neither did an adrenaline surge about going to look for a dog. With the dome and the window safely gone and their attackers in custody, they didn't have to worry about mobsters outside their door, at least for now.

"You were really zonked," Erik said as Ben dragged himself to the bathroom. "Or maybe I was. I didn't hear a peep."

"We were both exhausted," Ben admitted as he reached for his toothbrush. "But I'm still excited for today."

"I checked the shelter hours," Erik told him after they had both showered and dressed. "By the time we finish breakfast and drive over, they should be open. There's a whole process for would-be dog parents."

"I read it." Ben made coffee while they talked. "As far as they know, we have normal, safe, boring jobs without any supernatural stuff or Mafia hitmen."

"We do have normal, safe, boring jobs," Erik countered. "The ghosts and the Mob are extracurriculars."

"Like hobbies?" Ben joked.

Erik rolled his eyes. "Some people watch crime dramas. We just take that a couple of steps further."

"They want us to describe what our normal schedule is, and they'll ask questions about what we want to do, like hike, go boating, that sort of thing, to make suggestions about what sort of dogs might or might not like that," Ben continued. "Then we get to play with the dogs and see if we find love at first sight."

"We're clearly going to need to lie about our normal schedule, at least what it's been like recently," Erik pointed out. "Ghosts, mediums, magic, and Mafia shoot-outs probably won't make a good impression."

"I'm sure we can sound boring and normal if we really try," Ben replied.

"You know it might take more than one visit," Erik cautioned. "I don't want you to be disappointed if we don't find the right match immediately. We can go back as many times as we need to, and check some of the shelters in the area too."

"Is that just good advice or do you have a sixth sense about it?" Ben asked.

"I feel hopeful, but nothing out of the ordinary. Everyone I've ever talked to about adopting said that they knew when they saw their forever pup. I'm trying to stay open to possibilities."

Ben leaned in and kissed him. "You're going to be an awesome dog father."

"Isn't that the movie with Al Pacino?" Erik quipped.

Ben checked his watch after they finished eating. "They should be open by now. Come on, let's go!"

Despite knowing that the mobsters were in custody and their plainclothes escort had ended, Ben couldn't help checking for a tail as they drove. He didn't relax until they reached their destination without spotting anything amiss.

The drive wasn't long, but Ben's thoughts raced. "I know our lives are still dangerous, but I wasn't leaning toward a guard dog like a German Shepherd or a Doberman. They can be great companions, and if that's what we fall for, I'm okay with it, but I guess I'm just saying that I was thinking of a pampered pet."

Erik chuckled. "I'm fine with that. I was thinking along the same lines. And when I checked the dogs they had on their website, none of them looked like a hound of hell."

"Is there some way to make sure a dog isn't a shifter?" Ben asked. "That would be awkward."

"Mark Wojcik has a friend who's a werewolf," Erik recalled, thinking about their hunter friend in Pennsylvania. "He hangs out with Mark's Doberman. As for being able to tell, iron and silver would probably work. Some people say their eyes flash gold. But I think I've got enough psychic mojo to get a read," Erik continued. "I'm also thinking that a shifter wouldn't get along well with the regular dogs, so maybe don't pick the one all the others are afraid of."

"Do you pick up anything from your touch magic when you pet an animal?" Ben asked.

Erik thought for a moment before answering. "My psychometry works best on objects, not living creatures. When I touch a person, I can't read their mind. I'll probably be able to pick up on whether they're hiding something or faking their mood better than just observing them, but I won't get their whole life history."

"That's probably a good thing," Ben agreed. They had talked about Erik's abilities early in their relationship, and while Ben had initially been wary, he had come to appreciate Erik's insights as a secondary form of communication.

"With animals, it's a little different," Erik said. "I think it helps me pick up more on their mood than usual, and I've wondered if they actually read more from me than I do from them."

"I guess that will factor in to finding a dog that is comfortable with your 'something extra' as well as ghosts," Ben replied. "They say animals are sensitive to spirits. It would be nice to find a dog who takes ghosts and magic in stride. Don't want to traumatize the poor creature."

"Sounds like a plan."

Ben was glad that Erik drove, because he was too fidgety to concentrate. When they parked and got out, Erik came around and pulled Ben into a hug. "Relax. We will find the right dog when the time is right. It's gotta be easier than dating."

Considering the disastrous relationships both of them had before they met and fell in love, Ben had to concede that Erik had a good point.

"Hi! Welcome to the Cape Shelter. I'm Valerie. How can we help you?" A smiling young woman with a long dark braid greeted them when they entered.

"We want to adopt a dog." Ben hoped he didn't sound as nervous as he felt.

"Fantastic! We have quite a few to choose from, and new dogs come in almost every day. I just need to get you to fill out a form, and then I'll take you back and introduce you."

The shelter was clean and bright, with soothing music playing. He suspected that the volunteers and staff loved working with animals and had a commitment to the cause that gave the whole place a good vibe. Ben and Erik sat down at a desk and huddled together to fill out the short form. Valerie beamed when they turned it in.

"This all looks great. Are you ready to meet the pups?"

Ben felt his heartbeat tick up, and Erik squeezed his hand. "Absolutely!"

"We bring all the dogs in together so you can watch how they interact with other pups, and see them in an environment where they're comfortable," Valerie told them. "Hang back and let them approach you. That tends to work better than trying to attract attention or going up to them. Let them sniff you. You'll know if there's magic."

Ben tried not to flinch at the word, hoping for good chemistry but definitely *not* magic.

The playroom had white walls, plenty of light, and lots of toys strewn around the floor. A door opened, and a dozen dogs of all sizes poured through, leaping, yipping, and barking.

"Just one," Erik cautioned under his breath. "We can't take all of them."

Ben realized that, even if his heart said differently. He smiled because Erik knew him so well.

A sleek black lab was the first to approach, half-grown and leggy. He looked at them with soulful eyes and allowed a few ear scratches before gamboling off to play with the others.

"He's cute," Erik said. "Probably going to get a lot bigger."

A Pug waddled over, followed by a little white puffball that Ben guessed was a Shih Tzu. The dogs sniffed them and then moved on, apparently unimpressed.

"Guess we didn't make the cut," Erik observed.

After that came a gray Pitbull, followed by what Ben guessed was a Collie mix. The Labrador was cavorting with a young Golden Retriever that seemed to be all feet and tail.

Dogs raced back and forth, chasing each other and playing keep-away with toys. Some veered toward where Ben and Erik sat for a quick sniff and pat on the head before diving back into the chaos.

All except one. The gray and white mid-sized dog was an odd breed, with a short, shaggy coat and a face that reminded Ben of an old man with a beard. The dog stared at them from across the room, ignoring the other dogs.

Once the rest of the pack seemed to have forgotten about Ben and Erik, the dog walked right to them.

"George," Erik murmured once he petted him. "I don't know how I know, but that's his name."

George padded up and then sat, raising his head to meet their gaze. Ben reached out to scratch his ears, and George permitted it, giving Ben's hand a lick before inclining his head toward Erik for similar tribute.

"Wow." Valerie came up from the side. "That's a first. George usually keeps to himself."

Ben and Erik exchanged a glance, and Ben raised an eyebrow. "He's a nice dog. How did he end up at the shelter?"

"His owner died and didn't have any family to take him," Valerie replied. "It happens a lot."

"Do you know anything about him?" Erik asked. "That might let us know what George is used to."

"Sure," Valerie said. "His owner, Mrs. Thomas, read tarot cards and told fortunes down on the boardwalk. George usually kept her company in the shop. Some people said she was a little witchy, but in a good way. She knew she was dying, so she brought George to us before she went into hospice."

Erik and Ben shared a look, and Ben guessed that Mrs. Thomas's psychic abilities were the real thing.

Valerie shook her head. "I've seen dogs interact with all kinds of people, and they definitely communicate with us. But George and Mrs. Thomas had a special bond. I swear he understood every word she said to him."

"How old is he?" Ben asked, feeling more and more certain that George was the right dog for them.

"Two, still young but out of the crazy puppy stage," Valerie said. "Although it's hard to imagine him on a tear, he seems more likely to curl up in an armchair and watch a mystery on TV."

"What kind of dog is he? Will he get much bigger?" Erik scratched George under the chin, and the dog's tail thumped.

"Schnoodle," Valerie said. "Poodle Schnauzer. He's full-grown at this point, might fill out a bit, but shouldn't get taller. He'll be a mid-size dog, but he's got a big personality. He's very smart. Mrs. Thomas made sure we had all his papers, medical records, favorite food, toys, bed, and tags. He's up-to-date on his shots and check-ups."

Valerie smiled. "I'll let you spend some more time together and check back in a while to see if you have any other questions." She walked off, but George stayed seated in front of them, meeting their gaze.

"She likely named him for St. George in the Major Arcana," Erik said. "He's a protection figure, and a slayer of dragons."

"That fits," Ben agreed.

"He's associated with the Judgment card, which is said to reflect letting go of the past and starting over," Erik added.

Erik stroked George's back with the hand wearing a silver ring and followed up by lightly pressing a small piece of iron against the dog's skin. George didn't show any reaction to either metal.

"Guess he's not a shifter," Erik said.

Ben slipped off the chair and knelt in front of George. "Hey, buddy. You made a beeline for us. Would you like to be our dog?"

George's tail thumped, and he licked Ben's hand. His dark amber eyes met Ben's with curiosity and intelligence.

Erik joined them on the floor a moment later, and George leaned toward him as if to indicate that he favored them both.

"Are you seeing what I'm seeing?" Ben asked when an older woman's ghost appeared behind George. "Is that Mrs. Thomas?"

"I think we have her blessing," Erik said quietly. "I can't read George's mind, but when I touch him, I pick up a sense of calm and satisfaction, like we passed muster."

Valerie came back a few minutes later, after Ben and Erik had spent more time petting George and talking to him.

"Have you made a decision?" she asked, although Ben felt sure she already knew the answer.

"We'll take George." Ben grinned at Erik and the dog. "He's perfect."

She smiled. "I'm so glad. He deserves people who see how special he is. He's fully house-trained, likes to ride in the car, plays fetch, walks well on a leash, and doesn't fuss at other dogs." Valerie leaned toward them. "I think he'd prefer to sit on a comfy chair and listen to an audiobook, to tell you the truth."

"You said he came with some of his toys and stuff?" Ben thought that familiar items would ease the transition.

"Oh, yes. Mrs. Thomas wanted him to keep all his special things," Valerie said. "We've just been waiting for the right people."

They followed her back to the office, and George padded along behind them as if he had understood the whole conversation. Erik signed off on the adoption form and paid the fee, collecting George's collar and a folder with his papers. George waited patiently next to him, like he knew what was going on.

"Here you go." Valerie handed Ben a large box. "Bed, leash, toys, and all the rest. You shouldn't need to buy anything right away to get him settled in. I even put some of the food he's used to here at the shelter, so you can wait a day or two to run to the store. And if you have any questions, just call."

Erik and Ben thanked her profusely. Then Erik clipped the leash to George's collar while Ben stuck the folio into the box and followed them to the SUV. Just before Erik opened the doors, he and George turned around, looking at the same empty space.

"What?" Ben looked around before spotting the faint ghost.

"Mrs. Thomas walked us out," Erik said. "I think her spirit has been here with him the whole time. Now, she's entrusting him to us, and she's ready to move on."

George whined and gave a sharp bark, wagging his tail.

"She's gone, buddy." Erik reached down to scratch George's ears.

Ben swallowed hard, hoping he and Erik could make George as happy as his late owner.

"He picked us, remember." Erik bumped Ben's arm as if he could guess where Ben's thoughts had gone. "It's going to be okay."

"Go ahead and sit in the back seat with him," Erik said. "Let's get him a toy for the drive." He looked into the box and burst out laughing.

"They're all dragons!" Ben held up a somewhat bedraggled stuffed toy that George gently took from him and held in his mouth. "As in St. George the dragon slayer!"

Ben petted George during the short ride back to the apartment. The dog seemed unperturbed by the ride, looking out the window without much reaction. When they parked behind the store, Ben unclipped George's tether and snapped on the leash instead, helping him out of the SUV and letting him relieve himself.

"We're home," Ben said as George looked all around, canting his head to listen to something only he could hear, and then sniffing the ground with great interest all the way to the door.

When they entered the store, Susan greeted them with a big grin. Erik had called her the day before to let her know that the mobsters were in jail and it was safe to come back. "Erik told me you were going to the shelter. What a fine little gentleman you've got there!"

She held out a large dog bone with a ribbon on it and a stuffed llama, both of which she gave to Erik. "Just a little housewarming gift I picked up on the way in this morning."

"Thank you very much," Ben replied.

Susan bent to get a closer look at George and held her hand out for him to sniff. "Oh, you are a handsome boy, aren't you?" she fussed. "I think you're going to fit right in here." She looked to Erik. "Are you thinking he'll be in the shop, not just upstairs?"

Erik shrugged. "We haven't figured everything out, but that would be nice if it works for him. Ben might be able to take him on field trips some days too."

"He's officially my grand-dog now," Susan warned. "We're going to be besties; I just know it!" George wagged enthusiastically, as if he followed every word.

"We're going to get him set up and settled in," Erik told her. "Holler if you need me, but I'm going to be upstairs."

"Take your time," Susan replied. "He needs to feel at home. It's off-season, so we've had a couple of people ask about appraisals and some others do a little browsing, but otherwise it's been slow."

The off-season was another reason Ben wanted to adopt a dog now. Neither he nor Erik was crazy busy, if they could just avoid old scandals and mafia ghosts for a few weeks. It would be the best time to get George settled and into a routine.

"Let's go see your new home." Erik headed up the stairs to the apartment. George followed, unbothered by the steps.

"Here we are," Erik announced as he opened the door. Ben had George on his leash and carried in some of the dog stuff from the car. Once the door shut, Ben unclipped the leash and let George explore while Erik made a second trip for the rest of his things.

George got busy checking the apartment and thoroughly sniffing everything. "Can a dog hyperventilate?" Ben asked when Erik returned. "He's definitely going to have our scent when he's done."

While George made his way around, Erik put his bed in place and set out the toys. Ben filled his water dish and put dry kibble in a bowl, making a note on his phone of the brand and type so they could get more.

An excited yelp brought both Ben and Erik running to find George rolling back and forth on his bed amid the toys, wagging gleefully.

"He probably hasn't had his things since he was surrendered," Ben said. "They don't want the dogs to fight over toys or be possessive, or have toys get destroyed. Guess he really missed them."

George's papers said he was trained to ring a bell when he needed to go out, so Ben hung the bell on a rope from his box on the doorknob. After a while, George emerged from the bedroom carrying a dragon in his teeth.

Ben checked his phone for any missed work messages, then set up his laptop and sat on the couch, patting the cushion beside him for George to join him. George glanced at Erik as if double-checking that was allowed, then hopped up and circled a few times before lying down near Ben.

"You look comfortable," Erik observed. Ben turned on a soft rock music channel and George stretched before curling up again, as if to show he approved.

"I'll come over to the couch and join you after lunch," Erik said from where he had his laptop on the table. "Figured it was a good day to update spreadsheets. We can put on a movie later."

"Sounds like a perfect way to spend an afternoon," Ben agreed.

George slept soundly, and Ben took that as an indication that their new family member felt safe and comfortable. He followed whenever one of them went to the bathroom, asking for ear scratches and standing guard. After George slipped into the bedroom, Ben realized that the dog had repositioned his cushion between the door and their own bed, protecting them.

"Do you think George can sense the objects in the store that carry a little something 'extra'?" Ben asked. "Or the ghosts?"

"Lots of people say that animals have a sixth sense for that sort of thing, and given his history with Mrs. Thomas, I'd say it's very likely," Erik replied.

"I think we should take him to the festival with us this weekend," Ben said as they ate lunch. "That way he isn't alone in a new apartment, and he'd probably enjoy being out and about."

"I was thinking the same thing," Erik said. "You and I can take turns when we're not doing tours or presentations, although I suspect people would come just to pet the cute dog, no matter what we were talking about."

After they finished eating, Erik ran back downstairs to check in with Susan and give her a break for lunch. When he came back, he had a small silver charm.

"For his collar," Erik said. "I noticed he already has a St. George's medallion. I remembered that someone brought in jewelry with tarot symbols, which didn't mean anything to me at the time, but I thought it was appropriate to get one for George. It's the High Priestess, which is good for protection and intuition."

"That sounds like a good fit," Ben agreed as Erik fastened the small charm to George's collar. George shook his head, making his tags jangle.

"I think he approves," Erik said with a laugh.

They spent the rest of the day working as movies or music played in the background, giving George a chance to settle in. He trotted back and forth between the couch and the table, splitting his time between them, but truly relaxed once they were both on the couch.

"I think he likes it when our whole pack is together," Ben pointed out. George sprawled between them so that Ben had the head and Erik had the belly.

"He seems to feel comfortable here," Erik replied. "I'm glad."

George seemed a little put out that neither of them shared their spaghetti at dinner, but Ben had read that people food wasn't good for dogs. "Maybe after we go see the vet, buddy," Ben told George, who managed to look both insulted and sad at the same time.

"We should be able to keep his regular vet, groomer, and trainer, since we're in the same town as his old owner," Erik remarked. "That gives us history and keeps things consistent for him."

That night, George made a point of making a circuit of the whole apartment while they got ready for bed before he curled up on his cushion, keeping himself between them and the door.

"Good night, George." Ben gave him a last ear skritch before he got into bed. "I'm glad you're ours."

———

After a walk around the block with George and breakfast the next morning, Ben headed for the rental office, leaving George with Erik for the day.

"You didn't bring George." Jenny looked disappointed. Ben had sent pictures and let her know about their new addition.

"He's hanging out with Erik today. I wasn't sure how you'd feel about having him here," Ben replied.

"As long as he stays out of the 'pet-free' rental units, it shouldn't be an issue," Jenny said. "Especially not here in the office."

"He's got very good manners," Ben said. "I should get him a bed, water dish, and a few office toys. I think he'll be good company." He immediately added those to his online shopping list.

"I remember the tarot card lady." Jenny leaned against the edge of his desk with her coffee cradled in both hands. "I never held much with that sort of thing before you and Erik 'enlightened' me, but I walked past her shop on the boardwalk all the time. I think she used

'Madame Mysteria' for a stage name. Also sold teas and herbal soap that were supposed to calm and relax folks."

"Did you ever hear people talk about her? We think she might have been the real deal for having some psychic ability," Ben replied.

"Interesting. I never heard anything bad," Jenny said. "She was part of the Merchant Alliance, gave gift certificates for the charity auction, and I don't remember any complaints from customers. I didn't go to see her, but I have a couple of friends who did. They said she was very accurate."

The endorsement made Ben happy, glad to know that George's previous owner wasn't a fake.

"With all the spooky stuff you and Erik deal with, George should feel right at home," Jenny added.

"That was one of the things that made us sure he was meant for us," Ben replied. He didn't mention the ghost.

"How are we set for the autumn festival?" Jenny asked.

"Erik and I both have our presentations or tours ready," Ben told her. "I'm hoping we'll have good attendance. The topics are pretty popular, so I think we should do well. Our agents signed up for shifts at the booth, so we're covered. I've got a new banner for this year for the Nolan Rental Real Estate booth and a bunch of cute Halloween-themed pencils to give away, as well as a case of candy."

"I should probably personally sample the candy, for quality control," Jenny replied with a broad wink.

"Of course," Ben agreed. "And for anyone who fills out a rental agreement, we've got a variety of gift certificates plus a cute little eraser that looks like a house."

"I like it," Jenny said. "What's Erik doing?"

"He doesn't have a booth, but he's holding an Open House in the store with special sales," Ben replied. "I imagine George will be the life of the party."

"I really appreciate that you and Erik were on the festival commit-tee," Jenny said. "Gotta keep getting new blood. I remember what the off season was like before we started doing special events, and it was pretty lean sometimes," Jenny added.

Ben knew that the local library, school district, community college, merchant's guild, and art council all worked together to bring a broad variety of concerts, seminars, speakers, and festivals so that there were plenty of reasons to visit Cape May in every season, even when it was too cold to swim.

"That's one of the reasons I decided to come back and stay, even before I met Erik," Ben said. "It wasn't the sleepy town I remembered from visiting as a kid."

"I honestly think that fall is our best time, next to high summer," Jenny said, helping to sort brochures for the booth. "There's the Awesome Autumn Festival, the big Halloween bash that seems to last all of October, and a bunch of stuff around Thanksgiving with concerts and theater and special dining packages for people who don't do the family get-together thing. And then Christmas, hoo boy! We're not exactly Nashville or Dollywood, but we do Christmas and New Year's Eve up right."

Ben smiled at the community pride he heard in Jenny's voice. His aunt and uncle had been deeply involved in Cape May for decades, and that held Nolan Rental Real Estate in good stead when newer competitors tried to break into the market.

"The man who owned Trinkets before Erik bought it was also pretty involved," Ben observed. "Erik's tried to step into the roles he held, where there's a good fit."

"He was a nice man and did a lot for the community. Including getting rid of troublesome ghosts before anyone got hurt," Jenny added, dropping her voice.

"Did anyone take over the tarot shop after Mrs. Thomas passed?" Ben asked.

Jenny shook her head. "We expected someone else to come in—seemed like a natural fit on the boardwalk, at least for the summer. But it sold to a stage magic shop that sells all kinds of props and tricks."

If Mrs. Thomas had forewarning about her death, Ben wondered if she chose to end the shop's presence rather than risk her legacy with a new owner, especially if she knew she wouldn't be around to make sure things were done right. Ben's phone alarm went off. "Since it's quiet and I'm caught up on email, I thought I'd eat lunch at home and see how Erik and George are doing."

"Go," Jenny told him with a shooing gesture. "Take your time. I'll see you later in the afternoon."

"Thanks," Ben said.

Erik was busy with a customer when Ben got to Trinkets, but he found Susan and George in the break room, where George was eating a kibble lunch, and Susan had a sandwich and coffee. Ben grabbed his sandwich from the fridge and poured himself a fresh cup of java.

"How's it going?" Ben asked.

"I think George is going to be good for business," Susan replied. "He sits where he can look out the window, which means everyone can see Trinkets now has a dog. We've had a lot more foot traffic than usual."

"Nice to see he's earning his keep," Ben joked. "Jenny is okay with him coming to work with me and just reminded me we can't take him into any of the pet-free units."

"He gave the side-eye to the items on display that Erik says carry a trace of residual energy. Then he spent about ten minutes growling at the safe in the back room." Susan raised an eyebrow. The implication wasn't lost on Ben. The safe was warded, but like with the haunted window, it was the place for "spookies" that needed to be sent into isolation.

"How about the shop ghosts?" Ben asked. Trinkets had a few resident spirits who didn't cause trouble or want to move on, so Erik let them stay.

"I think they were checking each other out," Susan said with a laugh. "We had more cold spots than usual, always near George. He'd perk up, stare at nothing very intently, and then go back to sleep. I guess they decided they could co-exist."

"They say animals can sense supernatural energy," Ben replied. "And given his previous owner, he's probably more sensitized than regular dogs." He gave Susan a recap of what Jenny had told him about the tarot reader, and she nodded.

"I had friends who stopped in for readings, and they believed she had real talent," Susan replied. "Some of them went regularly, or at least whenever they had a hard choice to make. I don't know whether it's really something supernatural or just a way to open your mind to possibilities, but it worked for them."

Susan finished her sandwich and tossed the wrapper in the trash. "I'll give Erik a break so you two can talk."

She went up front, and Erik came to the break room. George wound around his legs, then went to sit under the table by Ben's feet.

"Everything okay at the office?" Erik grabbed his lunch from the fridge.

"Pretty quiet," Ben replied. "Getting ready for the festival. Bookings are solid through the holidays, so anything we pick up from the fair will fill in around the edges."

Erik swallowed a bite of sandwich and washed it down with some water. "Several of the people who stopped in today recognized George from the tarot shop and came in to say how glad they were that he's found a new home with us."

"Our dog is famous," Ben joked. "Maybe he should have an Instagram page."

Erik shrugged. "That's probably not a bad idea. As far as we know, George doesn't come with mobsters on his tail." Erik's *Treasure Trail* podcast talked about antiques and the store, but he avoided posting photos of himself or Ben online for safety's sake.

"Let's hope not. Bratva and the Jersey Mob are enough," Ben replied with a shiver. He sincerely hoped that both groups would steer clear for the foreseeable future.

"He definitely senses spirits and energy," Erik said.

"That's what Susan said. Just more confirmation that he's the right dog for us," Ben replied, reaching down to scratch George behind the ears.

"It'll be interesting going for walks, given how many haunted places there are in Cape May," Erik added.

"Surely Mrs. Thomas walked him around the neighborhoods," Ben said. "It's not like he's new in town. Maybe he and the ghosts have an arrangement."

"I'm looking forward to taking him with us to the festival," Erik added in between bites of his sandwich. "He's good enough on a leash and around people that I think he'll be fine. And if the crowds bother him, we'll just come home early."

"Works for me."

That evening, Ben and Erik took George for a walk on the beach. Despite the cooler temperatures, a lot of people were out, and it seemed like they all noticed George and waved or came over to greet them. George happily accepted the petting and compliments as his due.

"Let's see what he makes of Jon and Monty," Ben said as they approached the lighthouse.

George stopped right before they reached the lighthouse door and froze in place. Ben felt a dip in the temperature and saw Jon talking to George.

The door opened, and Monty stepped out. "I see Jon already found the dog," he said with a laugh. He joined them and fussed over George, who didn't seem to mind whether his admirers were dead or alive.

"He belonged to the tarot lady on the boardwalk before she passed," Ben told Monty. "I think he's going to fit in just fine."

"Seems like it," Monty said. "You wouldn't believe how many stray ghost animals Jon brings home. I'm not allowed to have a pet because the lighthouse is a historic building, but Jon's found a way around the rule."

"Are you ready for the autumn festival?" Erik asked.

"Oh yeah," Monty replied. "Not my first rodeo, although they change the event every year. I've got a couple of extra docents to help with tours, new brochures, and some key chains and snow globes for sale at the ticket counter. It's always fun teaching people about Cape May history. And Jon helped me pick movies for the classic film festival."

"Are you doing the ghost stories again?" Ben asked.

Monty grinned. "Sure am. We can't have a real bonfire on the beach for safety reasons, but I bought a very nice fake set of glowing logs, and I'll put them in a stone ring and have seats around it. Then I'll hold the story hour each evening. Jon's got a long memory, and he loves sharing with me. Ghost stories with a real ghost!"

"I'm looking forward to seeing how all the pieces come together for the events," Erik said. "Everyone's worked hard to make the festival a success."

Monty nodded toward where George sat, wagging and inclining his head to be petted by his new invisible friend. "I think George and Jon have hit it off. Stop by anytime!"

When they got home, Erik ordered a pizza. Ben picked a movie on streaming, and after dinner, they settled on the couch with George sprawled between them.

"I didn't realize how much we were missing a dog until we got one." Erik ruffled George's ears.

"Just thinking the same thing," Ben replied. "And with Mrs. Thomas's blessing, it really is a match made in heaven."

"The rain stopped, and the mobsters got caught, just in time," Ben said as he and Erik strolled through the Awesome Autumn Festival. George trotted alongside, well-behaved on leash despite all the people, unfamiliar noises, and tempting smells.

"I guess we could have told people we were shooting a movie, except for the real bullets and blood." Erik kept his voice low so he wouldn't be overheard. Ben elbowed him but laughed anyhow.

Many of the city's streets had been blocked off to allow for parades and special events like the costume contest and the pumpkin painting display. Along the sidewalks, vendors hawked candied apples, caramel popcorn, bratwurst sandwiches, lobster rolls, and clam chowder.

Banners along the way listed the special events and reminded everyone of the festival's sponsors, which included Trinkets and Nolan Rental Real Estate.

On one of the many stages, a group in full pirate regalia played a rousing set of sea shanties while a local cosplay group showed off their dancing skills. Tourists raised tankards in salute, and some of the braver souls tried to copy the fast-paced dance steps down in front of the platform.

Ben swayed to the music, bumping shoulders with Erik. The clear blue sky made the violent storms of the past several days seem like a bad dream. George kept a watchful eye on the crowd, but his tail wagged as he walked.

"Ahoy, maties!" a familiar voice called, and they turned to see Alessia. She and Haley shared a tarot reading and ghost whisperer stand, both dressed like pirate witches. "Wait, is that George?" She and Haley spotted the pup and came around to the front of the stand to pet him. "I knew Mrs. Thomas; and I wondered what happened to George when she passed. Looks like he found the perfect home," Alessia said.

"Ahoy right back atcha." Ben was pleased to see that their friends had rebounded from the strain of the recent danger. If George picked up on Alessia's magic or Haley's ability with ghosts, it certainly didn't seem to bother him.

"Please don't read my fortune," Erik joked, but Ben picked up an edge of truth in his voice. "I don't think I'm up to any more adventures for a while."

Alessia's face took on a dreamy look that Ben knew meant she was tapping into her gift. "Nothing to worry about in the immediate future," she told them. "You deserve a break."

"We all do," Erik agreed, relieved.

"Ain't that the truth." Chief Hendricks had come up behind them, with Susan a step behind. "I could go for a nice, quiet fall and winter, if it's all the same to you."

Susan gave him a look, but Hendricks didn't pay attention. George wagged frantically when he spotted Susan, who immediately reached down to scratch his ears.

"We'll do our best." Ben fervently hoped they could keep that promise, although the reality was out of their control.

"Have you tried the candied nuts?" Susan held up a colorful paper sleeve. "They're absolutely addictive."

"The huge soft pretzels are my weakness," Ben admitted. "Especially with the spicy mustard."

"I'm partial to the fried clams," Erik added. "Doesn't get much fresher than the ones here."

"How did your tours go?" Susan asked.

"We sold out two of the architecture walks," Ben replied. "People who come to Cape May love the historic houses, but they don't always know what to call the different styles or what defines them. And I'm pretty sure that quite a few of the folks on my walks went straight to the houses that are offering tours."

"The museum definitely leans into the fall décor," Erik said. "They had everything decorated and even offered punch and candy corn afterward. I was grateful that none of the paintings were haunted, and we didn't have any dangerous stained glass."

"Always a plus," Hendricks agreed in a dry tone.

"Then the '*Antiques Roadshow*-style' event they added last-minute was a big success," Erik continued. "Everyone wants to think they've got a missing Picasso in grandma's basement, or some other hidden treasure that's going to make them rich."

"Did they?"

Ben had his fill of missing artwork and found treasures, but he held his tongue.

"Nothing that's going to Sotheby's, but people did come with some nice examples of antique housewares, paintings by regional artists, and one or two old pocket watches," Erik replied. "Mostly, people had fun, and the owners got to tell their family history provenances."

"Think any of the people will show up at Trinkets and want to sell you their treasures?" Susan joked.

Erik nodded. "Absolutely. I've already got a couple of appointments."

"I've heard great things about all the events you two led. Not a surprise," Susan said, "but I'm aware you had more than your share of *distractions,* so I appreciate that you came through for us."

Susan didn't know all that had transpired with the warring Mob factions, but she knew enough to understand the danger and to realize that Ben and Erik had bounced back in time to fulfill their promises to the festival committee.

They waved goodbye to the chief and Susan, who headed off toward the costume contest. Erik and Ben paused to watch a pirate-themed sword-fighting performance, and despite the theatrics, Ben found himself clapping and cheering.

"Everyone seems to be having a great time." Erik watched children pick out pumpkins from a heap and proudly carry them to tables where they could paint jack-o-lanterns.

"And they are blissfully oblivious to how close we came to a mob war," Ben said. "As they should be."

"Everyone loves the movie pirates, but they were the Mafia of their day," Erik said. "It really wasn't fun when they came into port."

"One more illusion ruined by an accurate knowledge of history," Ben replied.

A busy stand sold tickets for Monty's lighthouse tour and evening 'Spirits of the Sea' haunted beach tour and story hour. Ben smiled, knowing that Monty would be accompanied by his very own ghostly partner and few, if any, of the tourists would be the wiser.

Since they didn't have to drive to get home, Ben and Erik stopped at the pavilion showcasing local wineries and settled in to try several different flights. The pavilion was dog-friendly, and George wasn't the only canine under the tables.

"I approve of this sort of spirits." Ben raised a glass in a toast.

"Works for me," Erik agreed. The knowledgeable bartender explained the backgrounds of the different vintages and what made them unique to Cape May. Ben bought a couple of bottles and made a note of others for future purchase.

"I know we've had way more excitement than we bargained for since we moved here," Ben said, "but I wouldn't trade it for all the peace and quiet in the world."

He surreptitiously snagged Erik's fingers for a moment before releasing them, but his heated glance promised much more once they were behind closed doors.

"Finding you was worth it all," Erik murmured.

Now that the storms had passed, the air was cooler, providing a much-appreciated respite from the heat and humidity. Ben lifted his face to the breeze, then felt a shiver when they passed one of the old Victorian houses. George paused and eyed the house suspiciously before picking up his pace to move Ben along and past them.

"What do you think the ghosts make of all this?" he asked Erik.

"I imagine they're used to it by now," Erik replied. "I think some of them are nostalgic, and the others just go about doing what they always do. The ones who don't like crowds make themselves scarce. Events go with the territory if you decide to haunt a tourist town."

They drifted through the crowd, greeting friends and neighbors and admiring the shops and homes that had gone all-in on Fall decorations.

They ordered cider-themed cocktails and settled on a blanket they brought with them to watch a classic movie on a big screen. Sitting side by side on the lawn, Erik covered Ben's hand with his. George sprawled between their outstretched legs, then rolled onto his back.

"I know I saw this when it first came out, but I definitely didn't get all the jokes," Ben said as the audience laughed.

"Or the innuendo," Erik agreed. "Although it's aged well, considering."

Ben thought back to when he had seen the movie in first run, and how much had changed since then, in the world but especially for him. Not just his job or location, but what he wanted out of life, and who he wanted to spend it with. Back then, he could never have imagined leaving Newark and law enforcement, or settling down with a man he adored and who shared a long-term commitment.

Ben leaned against Erik. "I like the now better than the then."

Erik briefly rested his head against Ben's shoulder. "So do I." His comment made Ben guess that Erik's thoughts had run along a similar track.

Despite their jackets, the air held a chill as they walked home. Music from the late-night bands provided a faint soundtrack. Any remaining party-goers clustered in the festival area, leaving the streets and sidewalks empty.

"That was a fun day, even if we did have to avert a Mob war to make it happen," Erik said once they were inside the apartment. He hung George's leash by the door and checked to make sure there was kibble and water in his dishes.

"Just another day at the office," Ben replied, although he could do with less excitement on a regular basis.

"For us, it really is," Erik agreed.

Ben turned Erik to face him and backed him up against the door. "Tricks or treats?" he murmured in a growl that he knew always went straight to Erik's groin.

"Both," Erik answered a second before Ben captured his mouth with kisses and let his hands roam from Erik's hard nipples down to his thickening cock.

"Then gimme sugar." Ben kissed and lightly nipped his way down Erik's neck.

Erik returned the kisses with equal fervor, sliding his hands down Ben's arms and back, then giving his ass a firm squeeze.

Since he had come to live with them, George had taken to sleeping in their room, but he didn't object when they closed the door from time to time. Ben figured George would settle outside the room, on guard.

They maneuvered toward the bedroom without really letting go, managing to shed clothing as they went before tumbling onto the bed.

"What do you want?" Ben asked, panting and painfully hard.

"Everything. All of you. Forever," Erik breathed.

"You've already got that," Ben murmured, sucking a hickey on Erik's chest where it wouldn't easily show. Erik licked the shell of Ben's ear, sending a shiver through him.

Ben made quick work of stripping off his jeans and briefs, then took his time removing the last few pieces of Erik's clothing.

"Tease," Erik breathed.

"Just getting you warmed up," Ben murmured as he slid lower to lick and suck at first one hard nipple and then the other.

"I'm warm already," Erik protested.

"Nah. You're really hot." Ben traced Erik's happy trail with one finger as he continued moving down Erik's body. He pushed Erik's knees apart and buried his face in his lover's groin, taking in the intimate scent of sweat and musk.

Erik toyed with Ben's hair and stroked the side of his face and neck, anywhere he could reach. He arched as Ben licked at the head of his stiff cock, giving himself over completely.

Ben put an arm under each of Erik's legs and pushed forward with his shoulders, spreading him wide. He took Erik's cock deep into his throat and set up a rhythm that had his partner moaning and trembling.

"Please, Ben. I want you inside," Erik begged.

Ben shifted enough to reach the bottle of lube on the nightstand and slick his hand, slipping it between Erik's legs to stroke his taint and hole. He teased Erik's tight pucker, circling the opening until Erik's grip tightened in his hair.

"Please," Erik's voice held a note of desperation.

Ben slipped one finger inside, edging Erik as he opened him up, resolved to take his time no matter how eager Erik was. "I'm not going to hurt you."

Erik groaned when Ben added a second and then a third finger, as his tongue traced the veins in Erik's cock or lavished attention on his balls, managing to keep his lover tantalizingly close to orgasm without pushing him over the brink.

"Not gonna last long."

Ben withdrew his fingers and shifted himself up between Erik's legs. He liked to be face to face, although other positions were easier. Seeing Erik's eyes as he came, kissing him through his climax, were two of Ben's favorite things.

He slid inside Erik's body slowly, savoring the feeling and making sure Erik was ready for him. Erik shimmied beneath him, trying to get him fully seated faster.

"Impatient," Ben chuckled.

"Just fuck me already," Erik panted.

Ben shifted his hips and started a rhythm, moving deeper and faster until he pushed Erik several inches up the mattress.

It didn't take long before Erik threw his head back, gripping Ben's hair so tight he winced, and climaxed, splashing hot come between them.

Ben finished seconds later and dropped breathless onto Erik's chest. They were sweaty and covered with jizz, happily spent. Ben listened to Erik's heart thud, matching the pounding of his own heart.

"That was…" Erik said.

"Yeah. It was." Ben pressed a long, slow kiss to Erik's lips, licking inside and letting him taste himself before he rolled to the side. "So much for these sheets." He used the top sheet to wipe them up.

"Definitely worth the extra laundry." Erik chuckled.

"Shower?"

"Definitely. *Getting* sticky is fun. *Being* sticky—not so much."

They took their time, letting the water and soap wash away not just the remnants of their lovemaking but the stress of the last several weeks. Neither of them was ready for round two, but that didn't preclude plenty of touching and groping, a comfortable intimacy that Ben valued even more than sex.

Later, when they slipped between clean sheets and rolled toward each other, Erik folded Ben into his arms. George had already fallen asleep at the foot of the bed, snoring softly.

"I hope we're done with excitement for a while," Erik confessed. "It's overrated."

Ben reached over and fondled Erik's cock. "I can think of better kinds of excitement."

"Very true," Erik agreed.

"We're here, safe and together. That's what matters," Ben agreed in a sleepy voice.

Erik's answering kiss was gentle and lingering. "Together forever."

"Forever."

AFTERWORD

One of my favorite things about writing a book set in a particular place is doing research to find cool, spooky, and interesting real tidbits I can use for inspiration or note as part of the location's history. Sometimes I change the name or adjust the details, but in other cases I use the real information.

Brent Lawson is one of the main characters in my Night Vigil series (under my Gail Z. Martin name). He and Travis lend a hand in a number of my other series, as do Cassidy, Sorren, Donnelly, and Rowan from my Deadly Curiosities series.

The Commodore Wilson Hotel is inspired by a grand hotel with a tragic history. The Tiffany dome was real, and to the best of my ability to research, no one actually knows whether it was sold in the liquidation or destroyed in the implosion. I'm hoping that a secretive collector has it tucked away in a mansion somewhere. Nothing suggests that it, unlike the hotel itself, was unlucky.

Weston Hall is loosely based on another real hotel that has been destroyed, as well as a long-gone English manor house, with a narrow stained-glass dome over a hallway.

Camp Wissahickon was also real, as well as the prior amusement park and the Coast Guard Training Center. So are the cement shipwreck, the observation tower, bunker, and the railroad tracks in the sand, as well as the famous lighthouse.

St. Expeditus by the Sea is based on a real hotel turned convent turned seminar location. For the purposes of my worldbuilding, it remains a convent.

One of the more flamboyant owners of the hotel that inspired the Commodore Wilson briefly operated an illegal radio station from a decommissioned minesweeper boat offshore.

The *SS Mohawk* is a real local shipwreck and a popular dive location. Lila's story is completely fictitious.

The Amber Room existed before World War II, although after being pillaged by the German forces, no one has seen it since, leading to conjecture about whether it was destroyed or hidden.

Cape May is rumored to be very haunted, and there are excellent books by a local paranormal investigator about many of the area ghosts. Haunted or not, the large number of Victorian houses are a treat for architecture buffs.

Cold Spring, the historic village and cemetery, also exists. South Cape May really did wash away in a huge storm many years ago and was never rebuilt.

Cape May puts on many seasonal festivals all year long, so there are plenty of reasons to visit besides the beach.

The information about the supernatural properties of the materials used to color stained glass hails from various sources. To the best of my knowledge, no one has reported a haunted stained-glass window or one with paranormal power.

The Tiffany Company did create custom windows for private commissions. They also made stained glass for mausoleums. Tiffany himself carved some stone angel statues as well as headstones (with lilies, a favorite theme).

Finding all these details and mixing the real with the fictional makes the writing fun for me, and I hope it sparks joy for people who know the area well and adds roots to make the setting feel more real. Enjoy!

ABOUT THE AUTHOR

Morgan Brice is the romance pen name of bestselling author Gail Z. Martin. Morgan writes urban fantasy male/male paranormal romance, with plenty of action, adventure, and supernatural thrills to go with the happily ever after.

Gail writes epic fantasy and urban fantasy, and together with co-author hubby Larry N. Martin, steampunk and comedic horror, all of which have less romance and more explosions.

On the rare occasions Morgan isn't writing, she's either reading, cooking, or spoiling two very pampered dogs.

Watch for additional new series from Morgan Brice and more books in the Witchbane, Badlands, Treasure Trail, Kings of the Mountain, Sharps & Springfield, and Fox Hollow universes coming soon!

Where to find me, and how to stay in touch

Join my Worlds of Morgan Brice Facebook Group and get in on all the behind-the-scenes fun! My free reader group is the first to see cover reveals, learn tidbits about works-in-progress, have fun with exclusive contests and giveaways, find out about in-person get-togethers, and more! It's also where I find my beta readers, ARC readers, and launch team! Come join the party! https://www.Facebook.com/groups/WorldsOfMorganBrice

Find me on the web at https://morganbrice.com. You can also find me on Twitter: @MorganBriceBook, on Pinterest (for Morgan and Gail): pinterest.com/Gzmartin, on Instagram as MorganBriceAuthor, on YouTube at https://www.youtube.com/c/GailZMartinAuthor/ on

Bookbub https://www.bookbub.com/authors/morgan-brice and now on TikTok @MorganBriceAuthor

Check out the ongoing, online convention ConTinual www.facebook.com/groups/ConTinual

Support Indie Authors

When you support independent authors, you help influence what kind of books you'll see and what types of stories will be available because the authors themselves decide what to write, not a big publishing conglomerate. Independent authors are local creators supporting their families with the books they produce. Thank you for supporting independent authors and small press fiction!

ALSO BY MORGAN BRICE

Badlands Series

Badlands

Restless Nights, a Badlands Short Story

Lucky Town, a Badlands Novella

The Rising

Cover Me, a Badlands Short Story

Loose Ends

Night, a Badlands Short Story

Leap of Faith, A Badlands/Witchbane Novella

No Surrender

Warm You Up, A Badlands Short Story

Point Blank

Memory and Malice, a Badlands Novella

Shine Tonight, a Badlands Short Story

Thunder Road

Fox Hollow Zodiac Series

Huntsman

Again

Silent Partner

Fox Hollow Universe

Romp

Nutty for You

Imaginary Lover

Haven

Gruff

Trash and Treasure

A Taste of Danger: Subparheroes

Kings of the Mountain series

Kings of the Mountain

The Christmas Spirit, a Kings of the Mountain Short Story

Sins of the Fathers

Kings of the Mountain Universe

Roustabout : Carnival of Mysteries

Sharps & Springfield Series

Peacemaker

Equalizer

Treasure Trail Series

Treasure Trail

Blink

Last Resort

Angels and Omens

Treasure Trail Universe

Secrets and Ciphers, a Treasure Trail Novella

Light My Way Home, a Treasure Trail Novella

Witchbane Series

Witchbane

Burn, a Witchbane Novella

Dark Rivers

Flame and Ash

Unholy

The Devil You Know

Signs and Wonders

Cursed

The Christmas Crunch, a Witchbane Short Story

Sandwiched, Witchbane Short Story

Ambushed, A Witchbane Novella

Midnight on the Midway: Carnival of Mysteries

Castle Magic: A Caynham Castle Collection

9 781647 950958